Disney PIRATES of the CARIBBEAN

DEAD MEN TELL NO TALES

Disney PIRATES of the CARIBBEAN
DEAD MEN TELL NO TALES

ADAPTED BY ELIZABETH RUDNICK

BASED ON WALT DISNEY'S PIRATES OF THE CARIBBEAN
BASED ON CHARACTERS CREATED BY TED ELLIOTT &
TERRY ROSSIO AND STUART BEATTIE AND JAY WOLPERT
WRITTEN BY JEFF NATHANSON

Disney PRESS
LOS ANGELES • NEW YORK

Printed in the United States of America
First Hardcover Edition, April 2017
1 3 5 7 9 10 8 6 4 2
FAC-020093-17055

Library of Congress Control Number: 2016953976

ISBN 978-1-4847-8719-9

disneybooks.com
disney.com/pirates

THIS LABEL APPLIES TO TEXT STOCK

The Beginning's Beginning

Young Henry lay on his bed, hands propped behind his head, eyes open, as he stared at the wall in front of him. Shadows, created by the lone candle flame that flickered in the breeze from the open window, danced across the room. Henry dared not light more than the one candle. He didn't want his mother coming in, not that night of all nights. That night, he thought, his brow furrowing with renewed determination, was *the* night. *The* night when he would change his future—and his father's.

Henry got up and walked to the far wall of his room. Every inch of the wood surface was covered with paper. There were pages torn from books written in obscure languages. Charts and maps competed for space, covering one another so that oceans blended into seas and rivers twisted onto dry land. He leaned closer, his long fingers brushing over several drawings of monstrous sea creatures. A large kraken, its tentacles wrapped around a sinking ship, was depicted in one. Another drawing showed a huge whale breaching, its eyes red with rage. Mermaids and mermen swam through blue waters, their lips pulled back to reveal fangs instead of teeth as they chased hapless sailors.

His fingers came to rest on one of the drawings. That one was unique in that it did not depict a creature but rather a man—or, more accurately, what had once been a man. Human eyes, full of sorrow and pain, stared out from beneath a heavy brow. But where smooth cheeks or even a beard might have been, instead tentacles grew. They seemed to move even in the drawing, undulating around the infamous face of Davy Jones, onetime captain of the *Flying Dutchman*. *Cursed to ferry the dead* and *Cursed to step on land once every ten years* were written across the image in Henry's twelve-year-old-boy handwriting.

Henry sighed. Davy Jones was no longer the captain of the *Dutchman*. Another had taken his place more than a decade earlier. Henry's father, Will Turner, now stood at the helm of the cursed ship. Henry's breath hitched in his chest as he heard a noise outside his room. Under the door, he saw his mother's feet come to a stop, and he heard her softly whisper, "Henry? Are you asleep?" He didn't respond. He loved his mother, but seeing her then might make him rethink his plan, and he had waited too long for that night to have it ruined or delayed. Finally, apparently satisfied her son was in bed, Elizabeth Swann moved on.

Only when he heard the sounds of his mother's bedroom door opening and shutting did Henry let out his breath. Turning his attention back to the wall, Henry took another long look at the two images that haunted his dreams and fueled his desire to learn everything about the sea. One was of a three-pronged Trident. It was being held by the mythical god Poseidon, and even in the simple drawing, the object's power was clear. The other image was of his father. A simple charcoal drawing, it was faded and torn. He was taller and his shoulders were broader, but the eyes that stared out from the picture were the same as Henry's; the cheekbones were similar. It was the only image he had of his father.

Reaching out, Henry grabbed both pictures. Then, bending down, he picked up the small bag that sat at the end of his bed. Throwing it over his shoulder, he blew out the candle and went to the open window. He paused, turning to take one last look at his childhood bedroom. He knew there was a chance he would never see it again. A small pang pierced his heart as he realized that he might also never see his mother again. But then he shook his head. It did him no good to think that way.

Henry looked again through the open window. In the distance, he could see the shoreline and the waves that glimmered in the moonlight. He put first one foot and then the other through the window. The time for thinking and wishing and hoping was over. It was time to act.

Henry rowed his small boat through the Caribbean waters. A full moon hung high in the cloudless sky, and warm wind, carrying the soft hint of salt, blew over the water. The sea seemed empty but for a pod of dolphins that jumped and played in the gently rolling waves.

Henry's shoulders hunched as he strained to move the boat through the water. His hair hung around his face, damp from the sea air and exertion of rowing. Despite the late hour, his eyes were bright—and full of purpose.

Suddenly, as though spotting some sort of sign, Henry stopped rowing. He sat for a moment as the waves lapped up against the wooden sides of his boat.

Silence descended, and for the first time since he had set out on his mission, the boy felt a small sliver of doubt.

What am I doing? he thought.

Then he shook his head. He knew exactly what he was doing. Henry had been planning it for months. Years, really.

He was going to see his father.

But first he had to find him. And doing that was going to take a lot more strength and courage than it had taken to steal a boat and row into the middle of the Caribbean Sea—even if that sea was full of pirates, sharks, and unimaginable creatures.

Standing up, Henry took a deep breath. He had waited long enough. He walked to the front of the boat and stopped in front of a large gunnysack. The thick, rough material did nothing to hide the shape of the rocks that filled the bag. A length of rope was tied to the sack at one end.

The other end was tied to Henry's leg.

Before he could think himself out of what he was about to do, Henry picked up the bag and unceremoniously dumped it over the side of the rowboat. For one moment, the bag seemed to float on the surface, as though not weighted down. But it was a mere illusion. The bag began to sink into the water, and as it did, the rope ran out with furious speed.

Ten feet was left. Then seven. Then five and a half.

When there was only a few feet left, the rope disappearing ever faster, Henry stepped up onto the boat's edge. His eyes calm and his hands steady, he took a deep breath and jumped into the water. Instantly, he disappeared beneath its dark surface.

All too quickly, the light from the moon faded above Henry. Darkness swallowed him whole. The water grew colder. As he dropped deeper and deeper, his lungs began to protest. His eyes bulged from the lack of oxygen. His hands clenched at his sides. Still, he remained calm. He didn't struggle. He didn't try to fight his way back to the surface.

And then, as quickly as his descent had started, it stopped as his feet hit something hard.

If Henry had been able to, he would have let out a triumphant shout. As it was, he could only smile as he saw what he had landed on: the wooden deck of a ship—a ship that was now somehow rapidly *rising* through the sea, carrying Henry with it.

A moment later, the ship breached with a powerful surge that lifted it above the water. Then there was a thunderous splash as its hull crashed down on the surface. As it settled on the sea, water flowed down its sides and out of its portholes. In the moonlight, the ship's scarred wooden sides looked like the bones of a giant beast. Thick algae and overgrown seaweed covered every surface. Ripped and tattered sails flapped until the wind caught them and they grew taught. The bow, carved into the shape of a fierce toothed beast, pointed into the dark night.

This was the *Flying Dutchman*.

Lying on the deck, Henry sucked in air, filling his

starved lungs nearly to bursting. He stayed like that for a long moment. Then he shakily got to his knees. He was still on all fours, his head hung low and his breath wheezy, when he heard footsteps coming toward him over the creaky deck. Struggling to his feet, he turned toward the sound and then spoke to the man coming out of the shadows. "Dad?"

Will Turner, cursed captain of the *Flying Dutchman,* stopped his slow walk toward Henry. His face stayed hidden in the shadows as he stared down at his son. "Henry," he finally said, his voice gravelly. "What have you done?"

"I said I'd find you," Henry answered simply. He took a step toward his father, desperate to hug the man he had met only once before.

But Will evaded his embrace, careful to keep his face obscured by the darkness. A mixture of disbelief, anger, and pride welled up inside him. "Stay away from me!" he barked. "I am cursed! Cursed to this ship." His tone, harsh and cold, seemed to slice through the young boy, and Will instantly felt a wave of doubt. It was not Henry's fault that Will had ended up captain of a cursed ship and crew. It was not Henry's fault that Will was not allowed to walk on land but once every ten years. Nor was it Henry's fault that Will had been apart from Henry's mother for over a decade. It had been a cruel trick of fate that had landed him on the deck of the *Flying Dutchman*. Fate and love and a good dose of stubbornness—the same stubbornness he now saw reflected in his son's eyes.

Softening his voice, he took a small step forward. "Look at me, Son. . . ."

The years had taken their toll on Will Turner. His once flawless skin and handsome features were now marred by barnacles that clung to his cheeks and neck. His long hair was matted, and his eyes were lined with the weight of the curse. His shoulders were more hunched than they once had been, and the mouth that had often been lifted in a lighthearted smile was turned down. He was the picture of defeat.

Henry didn't flinch. "I don't care," he said, once again trying to close the distance between him and his father. "We're together now. I'll stay with you—"

Will shook his head. It broke his heart to hear the hope in his son's voice. He remembered feeling the same intense passion to be with his father, back when Bootstrap Bill had been a cursed crew member of the *Dutchman* and Will had been a naive young man who believed in true love, happy endings, and good triumphing over evil. But those days were long gone. Now he looked at his son through the eyes of a man who had been truly and utterly destroyed. And he wanted his son to have nothing, *absolutely nothing*, to do with that life. He wanted his son to be free. Something he wouldn't be—not for almost a hundred years.

"There is no place for you on the *Dutchman*," he said at last, trying to make his point clear. "Go home to your mother."

"No." Henry wouldn't back down. He had waited so long for that moment. He had thought through all the possibilities—good and bad. Staying with his father meant the end of his life as he knew it. But what kind of life did he know? A life without a father? Besides, once he found a way to break the curse, they would return to his mother on land, a family reunited.

From below the rotting decks suddenly came muffled noises. Henry could just make out low groans and grunts and the sound of shuffling footsteps. Turning toward the back of his ship, Will sighed. "They know you're here," he said, speaking of his cursed crew. Grabbing Henry by the collar of his shirt, he moved him toward the ship's rail. Below, Henry's small boat bobbed in the water. "Leave before it's too late."

Henry struggled to free himself. "I won't," he said stubbornly. "And if you throw me over, I'll come straight back!"

"Don't you see I'm cursed?" Will replied sadly. "Cursed to this ship!"

"That's why I'm here!" Henry said, his voice cracking

with emotion. "I think I know a way to break your curse—to free you from the *Dutchman*!"

Hearing the sadness in his son's voice, Will felt his cursed heart break still more. "Henry—no."

But the boy ignored his father. "I've read about a treasure—a treasure that holds all the power of the sea. The Trident of Poseidon can break your curse!" Henry reached into his pocket and pulled out the soaking wet drawing he had taken from his room. Desperation filled his eyes and flooded his face.

Will forgot himself for just one moment, pulled his son to him, and held him tight for a beat. Pushing his son back, he looked him deep in the eyes. "Henry, the Trident can never be found! It's not possible . . . it's just a tale."

"Like the tales of you and Captain Jack Sparrow," Henry shot back, thinking of the WANTED poster that hung on his bedroom wall. It showed the pirate, his eyes lined with kohl, staring out with a mocking expression on his face. Henry had fallen asleep with that face in his mind for years. He knew the stories of the pirate, knew of his reputation as one of the greatest pirates ever to sail the Caribbean. "He will help me find the Trident!" Henry added stubbornly.

Will shook his head. "You have to stay away from Jack," he said, his voice serious. "Leave the sea forever. You have to stop acting like—"

"A pirate?" Henry finished. He put his hands on his hips. "I won't stop. You're my father."

Will sighed, the sound loud in the sudden quiet that gripped the cursed ship. Time was running out—for both father and son. The *Dutchman* would not stay above the water for much longer. "Henry," Will said, trying to get through to his son, "I'm sorry, but my curse will never be broken. This is my fate." Gently, he took the amulet that hung around his neck and placed it in Henry's hand. "You must let go. But I will always be in your heart. I love you, Son."

And with those parting words, the *Dutchman* once again sank beneath the surface, leaving Henry to swim to the safety of his small boat, a single thought burned into his mind: *Captain Jack Sparrow.* Despite his father's warning, he knew the pirate was the key to solving his problem. He would find that man, get the Trident, and then, finally, save his father once and for all.

Chapter One

Seven Years Later

Seven years had passed since Henry Turner had last seen his father. Seven years had passed since he had vowed to find Jack Sparrow and the Trident of Poseidon. It had been seven years of endless days spent working his way around the Caribbean Sea and endless nights of searching. Seven years of torment and frustration. And still Henry had nothing to show for it. All he had was his obsession—and a job as a greenhorn landsman on the British navy warship the *Monarch,* which, Henry concluded not for the first time as he looked down at the filth at his feet, was probably worse than any of the other torments he had faced in his nineteen years of life.

"Faster, you pathetic bilge rats!"

The sound of Petty Officer Maddox's voice shot down Henry's spine. For days he and the other landsmen had been working in the hot, cramped quarters belowdecks, manning the bilge pump. It was a thankless task. Bent over, faint from the heat and the intense smell, the soldiers worked to clear the water from the ship. Black with muck pulled from the wood and the sea itself, the water never ceased flowing. It was brutal labor that seemed without end.

Still, Henry knew his choices were limited. In the Caribbean, the British navy's main goal was finding pirates. Henry's main goal was finding a single pirate—one Captain Jack Sparrow, to be precise. So he had calculated that the best and fastest way of obtaining *his* goal was working with the navy on *their* goal. Unfortunately, his calculations had not taken into account that with little experience and no references—after all, mentioning his cursed pirate father would likely not have gotten him very far—he would have to start at the bottom of the naval ladder. That was exactly how he had found himself enlisted as a novice sailor and stuck listening to Maddox and his blustery talk of controlling the seas.

As Maddox barked his orders, Henry turned and peered out a small window. It let in very little light but it did afford him a view of the outside world. Through it now he could just make out the *Monarch*'s quarry. A small ship was a few leagues to their starboard. On its mast flew the telltale sign of a pirate ship—the Jolly Roger flag. But from his vantage point, Henry couldn't quite make out the name of the boat or decipher whose Jolly Roger it was. He glanced quickly back over his shoulder. Maddox was distracted.

Henry took a small spyglass from a hidden pocket in his pants and pointed it toward the window. With practiced ease, he adjusted the lens until the pirate ship came into view. Then he nodded. He knew that Jolly Roger, along with almost every other pirate flag found in the Caribbean. It belonged to the *Ruddy Rose,* not Jack Sparrow's ship.

"Henry, get back here!" Another of the young soldiers had noticed his distraction. In the bilge, one person's punishment was everyone's punishment. Worried Maddox would catch Henry in his act of insubordination, the other landsman nervously added, "You don't want to be kicked off another ship!"

Henry ignored him. "It's a Dutch barque, probably stolen by the pirate Bonnet," he observed.

"When are you going to stop looking for Jack Sparrow?" the other soldier asked. Henry's obsession with the pirate was a running joke among the landsmen. It provided plenty of opportunities for well-timed, and well-intentioned, teasing.

Henry's answer died on his lips as through the porthole he noticed that their own ship, the *Monarch,* had begun to turn. Henry could see nothing as the massive ship made its way through the smoke caused by its own cannon fire. Then the smoke cleared.

And Henry's heart lurched.

Right outside the ship, looming like a large gate in the middle of the sea, was a huge rock formation. Black stone formed a large arch that rose so high in the sky that it blocked out the sun. As Henry watched, the small pirate ship changed course and headed straight toward the arch, clearly hoping to find safety on the other side.

But Henry knew no salvation existed there. All that existed beyond that arch was destruction. Destruction and death. Or worse. And he also knew the *Monarch* was bound to follow the pirate ship right toward it.

Henry didn't hesitate. He bolted for the stairs. He needed to get above decks.

Unfortunately, Petty Officer Maddox thought differently. "I've warned you of leaving your post," he said, stepping in front of Henry. "Shall I show you the lash?"

"Sir," Henry said, trying to push past the angry officer, "I have to speak to the captain."

"What did you say?" Maddox asked in disbelief. His

face turned a deep shade of red, and as if he were a wild animal looking at prey, spittle collected at the corners of his mouth.

Henry didn't even bother to answer. Maddox couldn't help him. The only person who had any chance of helping him—and the entire crew—was the captain. And the longer Henry stood there, the slimmer the chance of survival became. Pushing the officer aside, uncaring of the consequences, Henry raced up the stairs.

He heard Maddox bellow his name behind him, but even the officer's shouting was drowned out by the sound of guns firing as soon as he arrived on deck. Unaware of the impending danger, the large naval warship was firing all its weapons at the pirate ship in the hopes of sinking it.

Captain Toms stood at his post, barking his orders with cold and practiced precision. Spotting him, Henry ran over. He bobbed and weaved through lines of soldiers until he arrived right below the wheel.

"She strikes her flag in surrender, sir," Henry heard the officer standing next to Captain Toms say.

Captain Toms gave a curt nod, obviously pleased with the report. "Chase her down. The British navy does not grant surrender to pirates." As the captain issued his orders, Henry saw him eye the rocks, concern flashing for a brief moment across his face. Henry felt a flicker of hope. But then, as quickly as the concern had appeared, it vanished. "Follow her in," the captain commanded.

"*No!* Don't do it!" The words were out of Henry's mouth before he could stop himself. They echoed across the deck. Instantly, the guns stopped firing and all eyes turned toward the wheel—and the captain.

In the beat of stunned silence that followed, Henry gulped nervously. Addressing the captain out of turn was a punishable offense. He hadn't thought that part through. Then again, punishment wouldn't matter if they were all dead. Taking his chances, Henry forged on, ignoring the cold, angry stare of Officer Cole, one of the captain's most trusted men. Once again, he addressed Captain Toms. "Look at your charts," he said, pointing toward a wall on which a collection of charts had been tacked up. "We're between three distant points of land with perfect symmetry to the center." He paused, hoping the captain would catch on. "It's a triangle . . ." he added.

"Stand down!" Officer Cole shouted as Henry took a step closer.

Henry stepped back. But he did not stop. "Captain, I believe you're sailing us into the Devil's Triangle."

Cole's fists unclenched—a little. The captain stopped scowling. For a moment, Henry thought he had succeeded in getting through to them.

And then the captain began to laugh. It began as a small chuckle but quickly grew into a guffaw. "You hear this, men?" he said, turning to his crew when he finally caught his breath. "This landsman believes an old sailor's myth!"

Henry shook his head. A landsman he might be,

but he knew what he was talking about. He had spent his life studying the myths of the sea. He had read epic tales of mermaids in Latin. He could recite the stories of men thought to be lost at sea only to return from the depths. He knew all about the mythical elements of the sea—including his own father. He most definitely knew about the various spots in the sea said to be cursed. "And I know that ships which sail into the Triangle do not sail out," he said finally.

Just then, Maddox ran up. "I'm sorry, sir," he said, trying to catch his breath. "This one is clearly disturbed! A boy who keeps lemons in his pockets!" Maddox reached into Henry's pockets and pulled out several lemons. The crew began to laugh.

Henry shrugged. "Lemons ward off scurvy," he said matter-of-factly.

"And what makes you think that?" Officer Cole asked snidely.

"I have no scurvy," Henry retorted. Then he looked around at the rest of the crew with a raised eyebrow.

"But all of you do." That time, nobody laughed. His point made, Henry went on. "Captain, trust in what I say. Change your course."

It was the captain's turn to raise an eyebrow. "You dare to give *me* orders?" he asked.

"I won't let you kill us all!" Henry shouted desperately. The captain remained unmoved. Frustration welled up inside Henry. He wasn't crazy. He wasn't trying to be insubordinate. He was trying to save everyone from certain death. The captain and his crew were the crazy ones for not listening to him. Every minute that passed brought them closer to the rocks, to the Triangle, to death. Before anyone could stop him, Henry leapt into action. He ran toward the wheel.

Just as quickly, the soldiers went after him. But Henry fought them off. He threw punches. He kicked. He ducked under one arm and jumped out of the way of another. Reaching the wheel, he grabbed it in his hands as he heard the unmistakable sound of a dozen guns being cocked. He closed his eyes and held his breath, waiting for the inevitable.

"Hold fire!"

Henry's eyes popped open. To his surprise, the captain had saved him. But as he watched, the older man approached him. Reaching out, the captain ripped first one sleeve and then the other off Henry's coat. "This is treason," the captain said. "Take him below."

As two soldiers grabbed Henry, he dropped his head in defeat. What did it matter now? If he was right about where they were heading, treason was the least of his worries.

As Henry was taken belowdecks and thrown into a cell, the *Monarch* resumed its course. Captain Toms stood at the wheel as they sailed through the large rock arch to the other side. To his surprise, the pirate ship they had been chasing was nowhere to be seen.

"Where did she go?" the captain asked.

As if in answer, the wind suddenly died. The sails fell limp and the sea grew eerily calm. An ominous silence fell over the boat. The sun seemed to fade, casting the *Monarch* into dark shadow.

"Sir!" Officer Cole's frightened voice broke through the silence. "There's something in the water!"

The captain slowly turned his head and looked over the rail. Sure enough, in the murky water below, he could just make out something floating. As the object moved closer, he saw what it was—the pirate ship's Jolly Roger. A shiver of fear went down his spine. And then that shiver grew to a quake as he saw a different ship appear out of the darkness.

That ship appeared to be more of a ship*wreck* than a functioning vessel. Its sides were torn apart, the hull open with the inside exposed, like a gutted fish. The figurehead that stuck out of the bow was so rotted and decrepit it barely resembled the woman it had originally been. As it sailed toward the *Monarch,* it faded into and out of sight, obscured by the darkness.

"Fire!"

Captain Toms's voice bounced off the rocks and echoed over the silent sea. Instantly, the air filled with the sound of cannon fire and gunfire as dozens of weapons targeted the approaching ship. But the ship kept approaching them, seemingly untouched.

And then the ship disappeared into the smoke.

"Fire again!" the first officer ordered.

The men didn't move as they looked at the empty spot where the ship had been only a moment before. "Sir," Maddox said nervously, "there is nothing out there."

And then, from the other end of the ship, came the unmistakable sound of footsteps.

The *Monarch* had been boarded.

Chapter Two

Inside his cell, Henry heard the screams begin. There was an old pirate in the cell next to his who jumped at the sounds. Henry backed up until he hit the far wall and then slid down. Looking through the bars toward the stairs, he could just make out the shadows reflecting what was happening above. Henry felt a pang of fear. For while he was trapped in the ship's brig, nightmares were coming to life up on deck.

First came the sound of footsteps. Soldiers pushed themselves back against walls and each other, looking for a chance to defend themselves. But there was no way to do so against this particular enemy. This enemy, the crew of the *Monarch* found out swiftly, was nigh undefeatable. And while Captain Toms fancied himself a man of reason and logic, what he witnessed defied both.

Because it seemed they were under attack by ghosts.

As Captain Toms watched, a pair of cracked gray hands materialized through the walls of his ship and grabbed a soldier by the arms. The man let out a high-pitched scream that was cut off abruptly as his life was ended by a swift turn of a sword. More hands followed. They came from everywhere—above, below, each side. Men were lifted off their feet like rag dolls and thrown across the deck. Others were pulled violently down, their bodies slamming against the wood. Guns and swords fell as the soldiers struggled to escape their attackers.

Through the chaos, Captain Toms saw one of his men drop the lantern he was holding into a pile of folded sails. They went up in flames, the light of the fire revealing flashes of black shapes floating about the decks. Within moments, smoke filled the air, obscuring everything.

And then Captain Toms spotted a man moving toward him. He cut an imposing figure as he walked, untouched, through the flames, stepping over the bodies of fallen soldiers in his heavy boots without hesitation or concern. As the man—if that was what he was—got closer, Toms saw that he carried a huge sword in one hand. At least five feet in length, the long sword caught the light of the flames and illuminated the man's clothing so that it appeared to glow red. Toms had just enough time to register the torn and faded Spanish Navy uniform before he found himself being grabbed by the collar and lifted off his feet. He stared into the face of the man holding him. Fear washed over him.

"What are you?" Captain Toms managed to say.

It was a valid question, for this was no ordinary man who held him. The face only inches from his own belonged in a horror story. Its pallor was disrupted with deep black cracks. The man's long dark hair seemed to float around him, exposing a large gaping hole on one side of his head. His ebon eyes, which bore into Captain Toms's, were lifeless.

"Death," the ghost replied.

Before Toms could ask any more questions, Captain Armando Salazar, the cursed Spanish captain who haunted the Devil's Triangle, ran him though with his long sword. Toms's lifeless body fell to the deck. All the members of the British navy—the ones on the top deck, at least—had been killed.

Turning, Captain Salazar looked at his men. They had taken a more corporeal form and now stood in front of their captain. Horrifying faces looked back at him expectantly. Each one of them was more terrifying than the last. All of them looked as though they had been blown up and crudely pieced back together again, as though they had just escaped the depths of hell. Grisly wounds covered their bodies. Some didn't have all their limbs. When Salazar ordered them to stand at attention, the army of ghosts lined up and removed their hats, revealing still more lesions. As they stood there, they appeared to be solid in form, but there was something undeniably *dead* about them—a cold, grim aura. This was a cursed crew led by a cursed and monstrous man.

"Straighten that line!" Captain Salazar ordered, walking down the row of men and inspecting them. It was a thankless task. No matter what the ghostly soldiers did to try to "clean" themselves up to meet their captain's high standards, they always looked a mess—their uniforms as rotten and fragmented as they were. It drove Salazar mad. His life had been about order and justice. And now he was trapped aboard a ship where order was elusive. Justice, on the other hand, was something he could have. . . .

Adjusting the collar of a soldier missing half his throat, Salazar addressed his crew. "By rule of the king we have provided a fair and just punishment. This ship dared to cross our bow—and so she will rest at the bottom of the sea."

He glanced at the rocky entrance to the Triangle. A flash of desperation crossed his pale face. They had been trapped in their floating prison, caught between life and death, for years, waiting for an escape that did not come. But Salazar would not give up hope. "I assure you," he went on, "your loyalty will be rewarded with blood. We will not rest until we have our revenge!"

As his crew gave hollow shouts, Salazar proceeded to inspect the ship for any more survivors. To his pleasure, he found none above decks. His men had done quite a thorough job. Blood pooled beneath dozens of slain soldiers. Peering over the railing, Salazar saw a few more bodies floating lifelessly in the cold waves. Silence had fallen over the boat save for the ghost crew's footfalls on the wooden floorboards, now covered in blood.

And then Salazar heard a scream.

The captain's head whipped around. The scream had come from below. With measured strides, he made his way through the bodies and down the wooden stairs that led to the *Monarch*'s cells. His crew followed, though most took a less conventional route. Some allowed their noncorporeal bodies to slip straight down through the wooden slats, while others floated over the water and entered the cells from the ship's hull. Another scream pierced the air.

Salazar made his way toward the screaming, then

stopped in front of two cells. In one, an older pirate stood, mouth open in abject terror, as the ghostly crew materialized around him. Salazar ran him through with his long sword, silencing him forever. Then he turned and looked in the other cell.

Henry Turner stared back at him.

Stepping straight through the iron bars that separated Salazar from Turner, the Spanish captain stalked over to the young man. He raised an eyebrow, waiting for the inevitable scream that usually followed his appearance. None came. Instead, Henry looked at him with an odd calm, as though he had been expecting him.

In a way, Henry *had* been expecting Salazar. Perhaps not him exactly, but something of his like, something too terrible for words. Listening to the chaos above, he had gone over in his head the various stories he had read about the Triangle—stories about something called *El Matador del Mar,* the Butcher of the Sea. And he had come to the conclusion that whatever was attacking the crew of the *Monarch* was not of this world.

He had been right.

That was why he could stand in front of Salazar and not scream. He could not help himself, however, from backing up a step as Salazar moved closer. And when the large man lifted his long sword, Henry *did* flinch. But to his surprise, the captain did not instantly run him through, as he had the man in the cell next to him. Instead, Salazar stabbed the long sword straight down. The tip pierced a piece of paper lying on the ground.

As Salazar lifted it, Henry saw that it was the old WANTED poster of Captain Jack Sparrow. It had fallen from Henry's pocket. Salazar saw the flash of recognition in the boy's eyes, and his nostrils flared.

"You know this pirate?" he asked, anger in his voice.

"Only in name," Henry replied.

Salazar narrowed his eyes. "You're looking for him?"

"Yes," Henry answered.

Raising the poster, Salazar brandished it in front of his men. "This is our lucky day, because the key to our escape is Jack Sparrow!" he cried. "And the compass which he holds." He paused to let his words sink in. Then he turned his attention once more to Henry. The young man shrank back. "No need to fear me, boy," Salazar said, his tone icy. "I always leave one man alive to tell the tale. Now go find a Sparrow for me—and relay a message from Captain Salazar. Tell him I will behold the daylight again. And on that day, death will come straight for him!"

His dead crew cheered.

"I'd tell him myself," Salazar finished, bringing his face mere inches from Henry's, "but dead men tell no tales!"

With a cruel laugh, Salazar knocked the boy in the head with the hilt of his sword, and darkness swam in front of Henry's eyes.

Chapter Three

It was yet another beautiful day on the Caribbean island of Saint Martin. Men in light suits and women carrying parasols to protect themselves from the sun strolled the cobblestoned main street, stopping every now and then to peer in windows of various pastel-colored shops. The air was full of the scents of sugar and spices. The sky above was a crystalline blue, and in the harbor, boats floated on gentle waves, their white sails bright against the turquoise waters. And, as was typical for a port island, there was a pleasant hum of activity.

"Stop that witch!"

The loud cry surprised several young couples walking. Turning, they moved out of the way just in time to avoid being run down by a woman wearing a torn dress. From her wrist dangled a metal chain. Behind her, giving chase and closing in fast, were two British soldiers.

Carina Smyth heard the word *witch* and her steps faltered. She hated that word. She hated that she was the one being called that word. She hated that because of that word, she was being chased through the town of Saint Martin like a common criminal. It irked her beyond belief. A part of her wanted to stop, turn around, and give the two ignorant soldiers a piece of her mind.

Instead, she kept running.

Catching sight of a large crowd gathered in the town square, Carina rushed toward them, hoping to get lost among the spectators. Muttering apologies as she pushed her way through the men and women, Carina kept glancing back to see if the soldiers were still in pursuit. To her dismay, they were. But they were losing ground. A triumphant smile began to spread across her pretty face. She was going to make it!

And then a soldier stepped in front of her. Young and inexperienced, he tried to block Carina's exit. It didn't work. She spun around him and then ducked under a wagon. Moments later, she was lost among the crowd.

Turning around, the young soldier found himself face to face with Lieutenant John Scarfield. He gulped. The lieutenant was known for his fierce temper. Tall and thick, he towered over the soldier, his eyes boring into him, asking a question without saying a word.

"I'm sorry, sir," the soldier said, the terror clear in his voice. "That witch escaped her chains."

Lightning fast, Scarfield's hand shot out and grabbed the soldier by the throat. His long fingers squeezed tight. "You're telling me four of my men have lost one girl?" He squeezed harder. "Perhaps this is why I was denied a fleet of my own, why I'm docked in Saint Martin instead of fighting wars in West Africa!" Scarfield threw the soldier to the ground and continued his rant. "The navy sent me here to kill witches. Now find me that wicked lass—or you'll swing in her place."

The soldier scurried away, three other soldiers

following close behind. Watching them go, Scarfield sighed. The day was not off to a good start. He could only hope that it would get better. His reputation, after all, was on the line.

Mayor Dix's reputation was on the line, as well. Standing in front of the newly constructed Royal Bank, he stared over the gathered crowd. It was his moment. With the dedication of the bank, he would solidify himself as a man of importance.

He had wasted years on that rock in the middle of the sea, his talents as a politician squandered. He governed over sailors and drunks and a handful of elite. He had to contend with the ever-constant threat of pirates and, of late, a rash of apparent witch sightings. He was tired of it all and he believed himself unappreciated. But that was going to change. Having a secure bank with ties to the continent meant more people of means would be attracted to Saint Martin. The mayor could rid the island of the riffraff and make it a destination for the wealthy.

Looking over his shoulder, he eyed the Royal Bank. It was a simple box-shaped structure made of wood. The mayor knew the outside was, well, uninspired. But what was on the inside was what truly mattered.

Turning back around, he raised his hands, silencing the crowd. "Today," he began, "we dedicate the Royal Bank of Saint Martin—the most secure banking institution in the Caribbean!" Behind him, two royal guards pulled open the bank's doors to reveal a shiny new vault inside. There were oohs and aahs from the crowd as they craned their necks to see. "Our new vault is five inches thick, stands as tall as any man, and weighs an imperial ton. Ladies and gentlemen, with this bank the town of Saint Martin enters the modern world, as no man or army will ever rob her gold!" He paused, letting the excitement build. Then he nodded to a skinny man standing inside the bank. The bank manager nodded back. "Open the vault!" Mayor Dix shouted as the crowd cheered.

Pulling down on the handle, the bank manager swung open the heavy door.

Instantly, the crowd got quiet. In the silence, Mayor Dix heard the unmistakable sound of snoring.

Slowly, he turned around. His eyes narrowed and his cheeks grew red. For there, lying across the top shelf of the vault, sound asleep, as though he had not a care in the world, was Captain Jack Sparrow. The infamous pirate looked worse for the wear. His clothes were filthier than usual. His boots were caked in mud, and his long jacket had several holes in various places. Some of the dark kohl smudged along his eyes had run down his cheeks. In his dreadlocked hair his usual assortment of trinkets hung at various lengths.

Physically, the man might have seemed down on his luck. However, at that particular moment, he was wearing a blanket of gold coins, and dangling from his fingertips was a large jug of rum. For a pirate like Jack, that was the good life.

"Pirate!" screamed a woman.

The shout jolted Jack and he woke, startled. "Pirate!" he shouted back. Rolling off the shelf, he landed on the ground with a thud. Then he sat up. Confusion crossed his face as he looked out at the gathered crowd and the guards, who had now taken aim at him from the bank's door.

"This may seem a peculiar request," he said, slurring a bit, "but would someone remind me as to why I'm here?"

In response, the soldiers cocked their guns.

"Wait, wait, wait," Jack said, hedging, "it's coming to me. Give me a moment to clear my head." He lifted the jug of rum to his lips and took a long swig.

The soldiers tightened their fingers on the triggers—

"Hold your fire!" a soldier shouted, startling the crowd. "There's a woman with him in the vault!"

Sure enough, in the vault a woman sat up next to

Jack. Like the pirate, she seemed confused as to her whereabouts. Her hair was disheveled and her makeup was smudged all over her face.

"He can't hide behind that trollop!" the mayor cried, growing impatient. Then he did a double take. The "trollop" wasn't a trollop after all. She was his wife. *"Frances?"* he said, surprise giving way to a burning hot rage.

Jack, however, was unaware of and unconcerned about the identity of his vault mate. He was much more interested in remembering just what he was doing inside a vault inside a bank on the island of Saint Martin. As he looked around for clues, his gaze landed on a set of thick ropes at his feet. They seemed to run across the vault, out onto the floor of the bank, and through two holes that had been bored into the back wall.

Jack got to his feet, followed the ropes to the holes, and peered outside. The ropes were attached to three teams of horses that stood at the ready behind the bank.

Next to them, looking nervous and antsy, was a mangy, motley crew of pirates, including Jack's old friend and first mate, Gibbs. "Right," Jack said, everything coming back to him. "Got it. I'm robbing the bank." He paused. "But there was one other thing. . . . Don't tell me. . . ." He raised a ringed finger to his lips and tried to remember.

"Shoot him!"

Instantly, the guards opened fire. As bullets flew, Jack dove to the ground. All around him, wood splintered as the new bank was riddled with bullet holes. In the back of the bank, the horses let out nervous whinnies and started to prance at the ends of their harnesses. A few reared up, chomping on their bits, and they tried to move away from the building and noise.

Inside the bank, the ropes attached to the horses grew taught. A moment later, the vault began to slide across the floor. With a thud, it slammed hard into the back wall.

Peeking through one of the holes, Jack Sparrow

saw that the horses were straining hard against their harnesses. The pirates struggled to keep control of the large animals, but they were used to sails and masts, not horses. They didn't know what to do.

And then the guards fired again.

At the same time, the horses pulled forward with all their might to get away from the terrifying sound. Jack felt the whole building begin to vibrate under his feet. The vibrations grew stronger and stronger. And then, with a loud groan followed by an even louder creaking sound, like a tree falling in the forest, the entire building began to move. The horses had pulled it completely free of its foundation.

A perplexed look on his face, Jack stood where the bank had once been. The entire building—not just the vault—had been swept out from under his very feet. He swallowed nervously. That wasn't good. Then he looked up. The guards had their guns aimed straight at him again. That wasn't good, either.

"This was not part of the plan," he said, rather obviously, to the guards and Mayor Dix. *Although it would help if I could remember the plan at all in a general sort of way,* Jack added silently. He was just about to open his mouth to try to talk his way out of the situation—a skill he was rather proud of having—when he felt a sharp tug at his leg. Looking down, he saw what he had failed to notice earlier: another rope was attached to his ankle. And it was growing taut! *Well,* he thought just as the rope tugged and he fell to the ground, *I suppose it's time for a new plan.*

A moment later, Jack Sparrow found himself being dragged behind the now mobile bank—in a rather undignified manner, if he thought so himself—through the streets of Saint Martin. Gold coins were tossed helter-skelter from the open vault and the hole in the building. Frantically, Jack tried to grab as many as he could. But it was a rather hard task, because at the same time, he was trying to hold on to the shaking rope.

Behind him, the guards continued to fire at the runaway bank and pirate. With each volley of gunfire, the horses went faster, frothing at their mouths, with their sides heaving. They turned a sharp corner, throwing Jack and his long rope in the opposite direction. Jack let out a shout. He was about to run into a house! Helpless to do anything, Jack found himself tossed through the window of the building and right into the middle of a family dinner. As though it were not at all unusual for a pirate to crash through a window at dinnertime, he bowed his head in greeting and grabbed a roll. A moment later he crashed out the other side of the building, just in time to watch the bank speed past him, the long rope taut. He raced after it, arms pumping, knees high, hoping the rope attached to his ankle wouldn't sweep him off his feet again.

To his surprise, as he followed the bank down another street, he saw that his little detour had somehow put him behind the soldiers as well as the bank. Glancing over their shoulders, the guards did a double take when they saw the pirate. Quickly, they stopped and turned their guns on him.

Jack gulped. That wasn't good. That wasn't good at all. He needed to find an escape route—fast.

CHAPTER FOUR

Swift and Sons Chart House was one of the oldest cartography shops in Saint Martin. Sailors from all over the Caribbean went to the shop in search of reliable maps of the seas and stars. Its reputation was a source of tremendous pride to its owner, Mr. Swift, who spent a great deal of his time and resources making sure that only the best of the best purchased his merchandise. And he also made sure that he never, *ever* had a woman in his shop. It was, after all, a well-known fact that women and the sea were not meant to mix.

That was why when he walked into his shop and saw Carina Smyth standing in front of the large telescope aimed out the window, he did not react the way one might expect a man to when finding an unusually beautiful woman in his presence.

"No woman has ever handled my telescope!" he cried in indignation.

Carina turned, an eyebrow raised. It was not the first time her femininity had been met with disdain. She shrugged it off. "Sir," she said, ignoring Swift's accusatory glare, "your celestial fix was off. I've adjusted two degrees north. Your maps will no longer be imprecise. Although you will have to start over with these." She pointed a long, thin, graceful finger.

Swift looked at the wall she pointed to. It was covered in maps—maps that had taken him a lifetime to create. Maps he had been selling for years as *the* definitive maps to the seas. And this silly girl was telling *him* he was *wrong*? He turned back to give her a piece of his mind when he noticed the metal chain dangling from her wrist. "You're a witch," he whispered harshly.

"Sir, I am no witch," Carina replied. "I simply made application to study astronomy at the university. . . ."

Mr. Swift looked aghast. "You what?" he asked.

"Am I a witch for having cataloged two hundred stars?"

Apparently she was, for once again, Mr. Swift cried out, "Witch!"

Carina sighed. There was no use trying to reason with the man. She would have to instead appeal to his wallet. "There is a blood moon coming," she said. "I simply need to purchase a chronometer. I'll pay you double for selling to a woman." She walked to a shelf and picked up the instrument. The small device used to measure time in spite of variations found at sea—like temperature, motion, and humidity—looked like a compass. She weighed it in her hands and then held out some coins.

To her surprise, instead of taking the money, Mr. Swift pulled out a small gun. "Help!" he shouted. "There's a witch in my shop!"

Carina opened her mouth to insist once again that she was *not* a witch. But before she could say anything, a man rushed into the shop—or, rather, pranced into the shop. He had brown hair full of knots and—she squinted to be sure—what appeared to be trinkets. His heavily lidded eyes were lined with kohl, and his hands, as he waved them in front of himself, flashed with silver and gold rings. *What in the world . . . ?* Carina had just asked herself silently when again Mr. Swift let out a shout.

"And a pirate!" he cried, answering her unasked question. "There's a witch and a pirate in my shop!"

"Well, then it's your lucky day," the pirate said with gusto. "Have either of the four of you seen my bank?"

A moment later a building crashed through Swift and Sons, ripping the shop in two.

"Found it!" the pirate cried as he grabbed Carina and pulled her out of harm's way.

Unfortunately, he pulled her onto the street—and right into view of the royal guards and Lieutenant Scarfield's men, who had up until that point thought they had lost Carina. Seeing their prey, the combined forces started chasing them. While she wasn't sure the pirate could be trusted—after all, she knew enough of the world to know most pirates *couldn't* be—she didn't trust Scarfield's men to let her go. So when the pirate took off running, she followed.

They raced down the street, turning corners where they could. Spotting a store with headless mannequins on display, the pirate grabbed Carina's hand and led her behind them. Then he stopped and posed so that he looked like the head of the mannequin. Carina did the same.

"Were you part of the plan?" he asked out of the corner of his mouth as the soldiers appeared and began to search for them.

Carina furrowed her brow. "I'm not looking for trouble," she answered.

"What a horrible way to live," the pirate replied.

The pair suddenly grew quiet as one of the soldiers

passed by. When he was out of earshot, Carina moved away from the mannequin. The pirate, while oddly dressed and odd in general, did seem to have rather solid street smarts. And she needed someone like that. "I need to escape," she said. "Can you help me?"

"That man called you a witch," the pirate replied. "And witches are bad luck at sea."

"We're not at sea," Carina replied.

The man nodded. "Good point," he observed. "But I am a pirate."

"But I am clearly not a witch."

"One of us is very confused," the pirate said.

Carina couldn't help agreeing. The man was clearly not of sound mind. But before she could point that out, the royal guards turned the corner. A moment later, Scarfield's men followed.

"Jack Sparrow!" shouted one of the guards.

"Carina Smyth!" shouted one of Scarfield's men.

"Stop!" the men cried in unison.

Carina turned to the pirate she now knew was named Jack Sparrow. He turned toward her. And then, together, they turned and ran up a set of rickety stairs. Reaching the top, they found themselves looking out over the town of Saint Martin. Below them, the soldiers began to circle the building like sharks hunting seals.

"We're trapped!" Carina cried. "What do we do?"

Jack looked down at the soldiers. Then he looked at Carina. Behind the dark liner, his eyes narrowed thoughtfully. Then he nodded as if making up his mind. "You need to scream," he said, and then, as though she were nothing of consequence, he pushed her off the roof.

And scream Carina did—all the way down until she landed, with a very unladylike grunt, in the back of a straw wagon passing by. Hearing her scream, the soldiers turned and took off after the wagon. On the roof, Carina could just make out Jack—now alone and safe—smiling down smugly at her. "Filthy pirate!" she shouted after him. But she had to admit, filthy or not, Jack Sparrow seemed clever.

Jack *was* clever. Or at least *he* thought so. Unfortunately, as he stood in front of the vault, staring at the single gold coin left inside, he wasn't so sure his crew thought so. Turning, he looked at his men. They had gathered, as planned, on the *Dying Gull,* Jack's dilapidated ship. Well, the word *ship* was generous. The *Dying Gull,* which was beached in the low tide of the shipyard, resembled an old barge more than a ship, with its cracked wood, lone cannon, and barely enough room to hold the crew—the very crew who, at that moment, seemed rather unimpressed with their captain.

"I told you robbing a bank would be easy," Jack said lightheartedly. He gestured to the vault. After all, he *had* robbed the bank. He just hadn't gotten any of its money. "Now line up to offer your tribute, men!"

Marty, one of Jack's original and most loyal crew members, looked up at him in disbelief. "You want *us* to pay *you*?"

Jack nodded.

"We want our treasure, Captain," Marty said, ignoring Jack's outstretched hand. "The treasure you've been promising us all these years."

There were nods of agreement and grumbling among the crew. For years they had been following Jack out of blind loyalty. They had followed him when he'd sailed against the British navy. They hadn't asked questions when he had gone after a ship of skeleton pirates led by the dangerous Barbossa. The crew had gone after him when Jack was captured by cannibals, and they had waited until he returned from the depths of the sea. They hadn't even argued when Jack later befriended Barbossa. And they never questioned Jack's dangerous journey to the Fountain of Youth, which didn't actually result in anyone staying young forever.

But this—*this* was the last straw. They had had enough. They were tired of being made fools of—for pennies, if they were lucky.

"We will no longer follow a captain without a ship!" Bollard stated, speaking for everyone.

Jack raised a hand to his chest as though struck by the pirate's words. "I have a ship, gentlemen," he said. "The *Black Pearl* has never left my side." To prove his point, he opened his coat. Inside, strapped to him, was a bottle. And inside the bottle was, in fact, the *Black Pearl*. But it was not the *Black Pearl* that had brought fear to pirates and naval officers alike. It was not the ship that had once been the fastest on the seas. It was the *cursed Black Pearl,* now a miniature version of its original form.

The crew stared at him. "The pirate Barbossa rules these seas now," Pike stated. "He has ten ships, guns full!"

"Let's go," Marty said, turning. The rest of the crew began to follow.

Jack grimaced. How could his crew have forgotten their conquests? They had found the Treasure of Macedonia together. And the gold of Midas. True, it had turned out to be nothing more than a trove of rotted wood and a pile of cow dung, respectively, but that was not the point. The point was they had done it together.

"Face it, Jack," Gibbs, Jack's first mate and the man he had *thought* would always have his back, said softly, "bad luck follows you day and night."

"Bad luck," Jack repeated. "Ridiculous."

"We know you fear your own sword," another of the pirates went on, "that you believe it's cursed—with intention to slit your throat!" In unison the crew members turned and looked pointedly at their captain's sword. It lay across from him on the deck.

Jack shook his head. "Afraid? Has ever a more absurd word been spoken?"

"Then pick up your blade and hold it."

Jack looked at the sword. Then at his men. Then back at his sword. He began to reach out for it and hesitated.

Then, in one swift move, he rushed over, picked it up, and hurled it overboard. Acting as though that were the most natural thing to do with one's weapon, he then turned back to his crew. "Problem solved," he said.

But the problem wasn't solved—not in the slightest. Before he could protest any further, the crew turned and, one by one, began to leave the *Dying Gull*. The last two to go were Gibbs and Scrum. "Sir," Gibbs began haltingly, "I'm afraid we've reached the end of the horizon."

Walking to the rail, Jack gingerly pulled the *Pearl* out of his jacket. He stared down at his beloved ship, a sinking feeling in his stomach. Where had he gone wrong? What had brought him to that point? He reached into a pocket and retrieved his compass. It was supposed to show him the way, point to what he wanted most. At the moment, it was pointing out to sea.

"They're wrong, Gibbs," Jack said, sighing. "I'm still Captain Jack Sparrow."

Gibbs paused, seeing the turmoil in the man's eyes.

He wanted to agree, but he couldn't—not anymore. Patting Jack on the shoulder, he left the deck with Scrum. Behind them, Jack remained, alone, one hand on the railing. Over the years he had out-tricked so many people and outmaneuvered so many situations. But perhaps his luck really had changed. Because he had no idea how he was going to get out of this mess.

Chapter Five

"The whole town speaks of you—the only survivor of the *Monarch*."

Opening his eyes, Henry Turner found himself staring up at Lieutenant Scarfield. Two British soldiers flanked him. Behind them, Henry could see nurses and doctors milling about as they took care of the soldiers who had been brought to the military hospital on Saint Martin. He closed his eyes again and scrunched his nose as a fresh wave of pain washed over him.

He didn't need a reminder of how he had gotten there. He remembered every detail with frightening clarity: the *Monarch* being overtaken by Captain Salazar and his ghostly crew; soldiers being skewered by nearly invisible weapons; the captain letting him go with the sole purpose of passing on a message to Captain Jack Sparrow; and then the long days at sea as he paddled his way to Saint Martin on nothing but a piece of driftwood. By the time he had made it ashore, he was delirious with thirst, hunger, and a good helping of fear. Things had gotten a little fuzzy after that, but he did recall trying to tell anyone who would listen about the ghost pirates and the Trident that could save them all.

His father! The thought of the Trident brought his real purpose crashing back. He tried sitting up, only to find himself unable to; his hands had been shackled to the bed. "Sir," he begged, "let me go of these chains. I have to find Captain Jack Sparrow."

Scarfield seemed unmoved. "It's my job to protect this island and these waters. Your sleeves have been ripped—the mark of treason."

"We were attacked by the dead, sir," Henry replied. "I tried to warn them!" In his mind, that did not warrant the label of "traitor."

Scarfield disagreed. "You're a coward; you ran from battle. And that is how you'll die." With those ominous words hanging in the air, he turned and walked away. The two soldiers followed, leaving Henry alone.

Henry lay back on the bed and closed his eyes. This was not good. He was in a military hospital, surrounded by soldiers, all of whom had probably been told to watch him with eagle eyes. How was he going to convince anyone of his story or innocence when he was trapped there?

"I don't believe you're a coward."

Opening one eye, Henry saw a nun approaching him. She handed him a glass of water. Slowly, he took a sip. While he appreciated the nun's confidence in him, he wasn't really in the mood. "Please leave me, Sister."

To Henry's surprise, instead of turning and walking away, the nun moved closer. "I've risked my life to come here—to see if you truly believe as I believe: that the Trident will be found."

Both of Henry's eyes shot open. He took a closer look at the nun. He now saw a torn and dirty dress peeking out from the hem of her habit. And underneath the covering on her head, he saw strands of wild hair struggling to be free. The girl was beautiful and young and clearly no ordinary nun. In fact, he realized as he caught sight of a metal chain around her wrist, she was no nun at all. "You're a witch?" he asked.

"I'm no more a witch than I am a nun," Carina Smyth replied, tugging at her habit. "Tell me why you seek the Trident."

Henry glanced around to make sure no one was listening. He lowered his voice. "The Trident can break any curse at sea," he explained. "My father is trapped by such a curse—"

The girl cut him off. "You're aware that curses are not supported by science?" she asked.

Henry shrugged. "Neither are ghosts," he pointed out. *But I've seen them,* he added silently.

"So you've gone mad?" Carina asked. Then she sighed. "I never should have come here. . . ."

"Then why did you?" Henry asked.

Carina started to leave but paused, thinking better of it. She *had* come for a reason. It seemed wrong to just walk away. "I need to get off this island," she said. "To solve the Map—"

"No Man Can Read?" Henry finished, his excitement growing. How did this girl know about the map supposedly left behind by Poseidon himself?

She seemed to be wondering the same thing about him. "You've read the ancient texts?"

Henry nodded. "In each language they were written," he replied with no hint of arrogance. "And no man has ever seen this map."

"Luckily, I'm a woman," Carina retorted. She reached into her habit and pulled out a book. It was worn and weathered with age, its pages brittle and its cover torn. In the center of the cover, hovering over a picture of a sea of stars, was a large red ruby. Henry found himself reaching for the book, but Carina pulled it back. "This is the diary of Galileo Galilei. He spent his life looking for the map."

Henry widened his eyes in wonder. He knew who Galileo Galilei was—the astronomer and scientist who had invented the spyglass to scan the stars.

But apparently, that was *not* the reason he had invented it. At least, not according to Carina. He had invented it, she explained, to search for the *map*.

"You're saying the Map No Man Can Read is hidden in the stars?" Henry asked, trying to wrap his head around what the girl was saying.

She nodded. "Soon there will be a blood moon. Only then will the map be read—and the Trident found."

Henry stared at the girl, dumbfounded. "Who *are* you?" he finally asked.

"Carina Smyth!"

Scarfield's voice echoed through the room. Henry saw that the lieutenant was walking toward them—with more men trailing behind, hands on their swords.

Above Henry, Carina ever so stealthily pulled a small metal pick out of a pocket in her habit. "If you wish to save your father," she whispered to Henry, her lips barely moving as she dropped the pick into his hand, "you'll have to save me. Find us a ship—and the Trident will be ours."

"Turn to me, witch!" Scarfield ordered, closing in on them.

Instantly, Carina took off running. Behind her, Scarfield let out a curse. He signaled to his men, and they went after her.

Henry didn't hesitate. As Carina led the men in a chase around the room, he freed himself from his shackles. Dropping them to the floor, he scanned the room for a way out. He caught sight of Carina, standing in front of one of the large windows. Scarfield and his men had her cornered. Henry and the girl exchanged looks, and then, before anyone could stop him, Henry slipped through another window. Behind him he heard the soldiers shout in alarm. But it was too late. He was free. And when he reunited with Carina, he would be one step closer to rescuing his father. It seemed his luck had taken a turn for the better.

Jack Sparrow's luck, however, had not. After his crew had abandoned him, he had tried to prove—at least to himself—that he was not unlucky. But he had failed miserably. First he had tried to rob a coach on the outskirts of town only to have it drive right by him. Then it had begun to rain. And when he had finally made it back into town and wandered into a local watering hole, looking for a beverage to quench his thirst, the barkeep had asked him to show him his silver, of which he had none. The only thing in his pockets, it turned out, was his compass.

"Well, do you want that drink or not?" the barkeep asked, watching Jack.

Jack looked down at the compass in his hand, torn between his thirst and his prized possession. Before he could make a decision, a fisherman wandered in and plopped his catch down on the bar next to Jack. Sticking out of the net was Jack's sword.

"Would you look at that?" the fisherman said, unaware of what his haul meant to the pirate next to him. "A fish stabbed itself with this here sword. I'll sell it to the navy! How's that for luck?"

With a shout, Jack reached over and grabbed the sword. He flung it across the bar. It hit a WANTED poster hanging on the far wall with an audible twang, the point firmly embedded right between the eyes of one Captain Jack Sparrow. With a sigh, Jack threw the compass on the bar. "The bottle," he said.

As the barkeep handed him the brown bottle, the compass began to vibrate. Slight at first, the vibrations grew stronger and stronger. The men sitting at the bar looked up in confusion while Jack jumped back, fear in his eyes. Bottles and glassware began to fall to the ground and shatter as the small earthquake continued.

Jack had made a mistake—a big one. Nervously, he reached out to take back his compass—and hopefully right a wrong—but the barkeep snatched it up. Instantly, the quaking stopped. Shrugging, the man threw the compass over his shoulder. It landed in the middle of a pile of jewelry and trinkets collected in the same manner the compass had been—as payment.

Jack sighed and lifted the bottle to his lips. "The pirate's life," he said quietly. *At least, it used to be,* he added silently before taking a long, deep drink.

Under a dark sky, the *Silent Mary* sailed through the Devil's Triangle. On its decks, the ghostly crew worked, scrubbing the boards that would never come clean and mending sails that could never be mended. They would never stop trying. It was captain's orders, after all.

Up at the wheelhouse, Captain Salazar looked over the quiet sea, his eyes hard. He had been staring at the same sea for a lifetime. The same skeletal gulls hovered over their ship. The same dead men manned his crew. The same feeling of betrayal filled his unbeating heart. The curse he had been under was endless and excruciating. At his sides, his hands clenched tightly, anger coursing through him instead of blood.

And then he saw something. The ship's wheel moved ever so slightly. Salazar narrowed his eyes and took a step closer. The wheel moved again. On its own, it began to steer the ship in a new direction. Sensing the change in course, the crew looked up and saw their captain standing a distance from the wheel. Curious, they stepped forward.

"Sir," Salazar's lieutenant, a ghost named Lesaro, began, "what's happening?"

The captain did not answer at first. Instead, he looked out toward the horizon. At that moment, the highest peak of the Devil's Triangle crumbled, revealing the shining sun behind it. Then the entire arch began to fall apart, rocks tumbling into the sea. There could be only one reason for this change in scenery. Could Jack Sparrow be so foolish? As the thought crossed his mind, the ship turned still further, the bow now aimed toward the distant horizon. A small smile began to spread across Salazar's face. It appeared the pirate *could* be that foolish. "Jack Sparrow has given away the key!" he shouted over his shoulder.

He could hear his crew members muttering among themselves behind him. Some were confused, others excited even though they didn't know exactly what that meant. Moving to stand beside him, a ghost named Santos pointed over the rail. "Sir, what is that?" he asked in confusion.

Salazar's small smile grew into a bigger one. "Daylight," he said. "After all these years, it's time!"

The sunlight appeared to be growing wider and

wider until, with a flash, it seemed to create a hole in what had been up until then an invisible border.

Captain Salazar wasted no time. "Hard to starboard!" he shouted to his men. "We'll sail to the edge and cross with the light!"

"Aye, sir," Lieutenant Lesaro responded. Turning to the crew, he gave the order. "All hands full and make more sail!"

As the men rushed to their posts and began to prepare the ship, Captain Salazar stared straight ahead. The daylight was moving closer and closer. The Devil's Triangle was no more. The ship picked up speed as its sails caught the wind, and then, with a whoosh, it burst through the hole of sunlight and into the sea beyond.

There was a moment of silence as the ghostly crew of the *Silent Mary* stared at the sea around them. The dark sky of the Triangle had been replaced with a bright blue one. The rougher seas had calmed.

"We're free!" Lieutenant Lesaro's shout echoed

over the water as the crew cheered. Standing by the wheel, Captain Salazar nodded. It was true. They were free—finally.

"My very dead men," he said, turning to his crew with a triumphant smile, "the sea is ours! It is time to go hunt a pirate!"

As his cruel laugh bounced off the waves, the *Silent Mary* set a new course. Salazar was going after Jack Sparrow, and he wouldn't stop hunting pirates until he found him—and made him pay for every moment Salazar had been trapped in his watery hell. He stared into the distance and spotted the telltale Jolly Roger of a pirate ship. It looked like he could start his hunting immediately. The pirate's way of life was over.

Chapter Six

Night had fallen on the isle of Saint Martin. Unaware of the new danger stalking the seas, its citizens tucked themselves into bed for the night, cozy in their ignorance. In the sky hung a large full moon. But it was no ordinary full moon. It shone bright red in the dark sky—a blood moon.

Inside her cell, Carina was making calculations on the wall by the light of the ominous moon. Time was running out. She didn't need a timepiece to know that. She sensed it in her bones. Her chance at finding the Trident and discovering the true meaning of Galileo's diary was slipping from her grasp. A wave of desperation flooded over her, but as quickly as it overcame her, she brushed it off. She had come up against harder odds and beaten them in the past. She could do it again. She just needed to think harder. Holding the book up to the moonlight, she turned it this way and that. "Just because you can't see something," she said softly to herself, "doesn't mean it's not there. . . ." Her voice trailed off as she looked down at the brilliant red ruby on the cover of the diary.

The moonlight caused it to shimmer enticingly, and Carina was unable to stop herself from pulling off the ruby. She had done it many times before, but never in a prison cell and never under the light of a blood moon, or more scientifically speaking, a lunar eclipse. To her surprise, as the light shone through the ruby, words that had been invisible began to appear on the cover of the diary. "'To release the power of the sea, all must divide,'" she read.

Then she noticed that the ruby had illuminated something else in the illustration of the waves—a small island.

A pair of soldiers made their way down the prison hall. They stopped in front of Lieutenant Scarfield, who was standing guard at the front. Scarfield and his men had brought in two important prisoners that day—Carina and, as luck would have it, Jack Sparrow, the latter having gotten so drunk at the local tavern he had been unable to fight off the soldiers who stumbled upon him. The lieutenant now refused to leave the prison, even though it was heavily guarded and it was below his station to stand watch. He had let the witch and the pirate slip out of his grasp too many times that day to take any chances. And he was still furious that he had managed to lose the traitor, Henry Turner.

"Sir," one of the soldiers said, addressing the lieutenant, "we have reports of ships burning at sea. An unknown enemy has taken to these waters."

"Pirates?" Scarfield asked.

The soldiers shook their heads. "Something else," the first officer answered.

While the trio continued to discuss the situation,

a lone guard in a red coat made his way quickly down the hall of the dark prison. The guard's cap was pulled low over his eyes, obscuring his features. He came to a stop in front of one of the dankest, dirtiest cells. Then he stepped up to the bars.

"I need to speak with you," he whispered. As he leaned forward, the moonlight illuminated his features, revealing him to be Henry Turner. He waited with bated breath for an answer from inside the cell. Suddenly, an arm went around Henry's neck, pulling him tightly against the bars.

"Hand me your sword."

Henry shook his head. "I have no weapon."

"What kind of soldier has no sword?" Jack asked, surprised.

"I'm currently wanted for treason."

There was a pause. "So not a very good kind," the pirate observed.

Henry shrugged. He couldn't argue with that. Although, if he had had the time or inclination, he might have pointed out that while he might not be a good soldier, at least he wasn't locked up. "I've come to see the pirate Jack Sparrow," Henry said instead, hoping his words might put an end to the uncomfortable position he currently found himself in.

That seemed to do the trick. The arm loosened around his neck. Quickly, Henry stepped back. As he caught his breath, he finally had the chance to look at the pirate he had heard so much about. "Where is your ship?" he asked. "Your crew? Your . . . pants?"

Sure enough, Jack was without his pants. He shrugged. "A great pirate doesn't require such intricacies."

Henry was horrified. "Do you know how long I've been waiting for this moment?" he asked. "I've risked everything to be here! Are you sure you're *the* Jack Sparrow?"

"We both know who I am. The question remains"—the pirate took a step closer to the bars and stared Henry down with kohl-rimmed eyes—"who are *you*?"

Henry hesitated. "My name is Henry Turner," he

finally said. "Son of Will Turner and Elizabeth Swann."

Jack frowned. He pulled back and then reached through the bars, turning Henry's head one way, then the other, studying him. "Ecch!" he finally said, apparently seeing the resemblance. "So you are the evil spawn of them two?" Henry nodded, ripping his face free of the pirate's long ringed fingers. "Does Mommy ever ask about me?"

"Never," Henry said, surprised by Jack's question.

"Did she call my name in her sleep?" Jack pressed.

Henry shook his head. "She never spoke of you."

Letting out a sigh, Jack finally moved on—sort of. "Are you sure we're talking about the same people? He's a cursed eunuch, she's golden-haired and stubborn, pouty lips, neck like a giraffe, and two of those wonderful—"

"Yes, yes, it's her!" Henry interrupted, his voice rising. He cringed. Had the pirate no sense of decency? That was Henry's *mother* he was talking about. He lowered his voice and went on. "I need you to listen, Jack, because at the moment, you're all I've got! I found a way to save my father. There is one thing that can break his curse and free him from the *Dutchman*—the Trident of Poseidon."

"A treasure to be found with a Map No Man Can Read?" Jack asked after a moment. He shrugged. "Never heard of it."

Henry frowned. Clearly the pirate *had* heard of it, or else he wouldn't have known exactly how to find the treasure. A part of Henry wanted to walk away and leave the snarky pirate to rot in his cell. But while that might have brought him some sense of satisfaction, he knew he couldn't.

"There is a girl in this prison who holds the map," he continued. "Look to that window, Jack—the moon has turned to blood. The Trident will be found. . . ." He stopped as the sound of snoring filled the cell. Jack had pretended to fall asleep.

Slowly, Jack turned from the window. "Sorry," he said, feigning indifference. "Were you still talking? I believe I nodded off. . . ." He watched Henry's face fall before turning his back on the boy, the conversation over.

Dejected, Henry spun on his heel to leave. But then he paused. He had one last card to play. "There's one other thing," he said over his shoulder. "A message from someone you know. A captain named . . . Salazar."

Henry's words did the trick. Jack's face grew pale, and he struggled to stop his hands from shaking. "I once knew a Spaniard named something in Spanish," he said, trying to keep his voice light.

"El Matador del Mar!" Henry said, exasperated by Jack's inability to be serious. "The Butcher of the Sea!"

Jack Sparrow shook his head. He knew that was impossible. Salazar was dead. Sunk to the bottom of the sea. There was no feasible or conceivable way that he could be coming for him.

Apparently, however, it was quite feasible. "He's coming for you, Jack, to seek revenge as the dead man's tale is told."

"I don't believe you," Jack said, his tone not convincing either of them. He leaned a bit closer. "What did he say?" he whispered.

"He said your compass was the key to his escape," Henry replied.

Jack reached for the compass only to remember that it was not there. It was, to his knowledge, still sitting behind the bar among a pile of trinkets and gold.

Unaware that one of Jack's most prized possessions was no longer with him, Henry went on, his words oddly prophetic. "An army of dead are coming straight for you, Jack. The Trident of Poseidon is your only hope. So . . . do we have an accord?" He held out his hand and waited.

Jack looked at the young man staring at him hopefully. He saw so much of Will in the boy's eyes. The hope, the trust, the drive. He had always found those qualities in Will Turner irksome. He found them equally irksome in Will's son. Still, the boy had a point. Jack had lost his compass. The *Black Pearl* was a useless toy. His prospects were, well, dim. Finally, he gave a small nod. "Do you have any silver?" he asked, taking Henry's hand. "Because we're going to need a crew." He looked down at his outfit—or lack thereof. "And pants."

Chapter Seven

Life aboard the *Queen Anne's Revenge* was good. While Jack's luck had taken a decided turn for the worse, Captain Hector Barbossa's luck had taken a decided turn for the better—the much, *much* better. Since parting ways with Jack and his shenanigans, Barbossa had taken over the pirate world. He no longer had just one boat; he had a fleet. He no longer had just a crew; he had *crews*. His name was whispered with fear in ports across the Caribbean, and when his Jolly Roger was spotted at sea, pirates and soldiers alike knew it was only a matter of time before they were conquered.

Barbossa had just concluded another successful round of pillaging and plundering and brought the *Queen Anne's Revenge* into port. The ship looked less like a ship and more like the inside of an antique shop or museum. Countless statues, yards of silk, dozens of rugs, and furniture decorated with pure gold were stacked helter-skelter across the wooden decking. His men had already passed the majority of the day spending their spoils and had returned to the ship to continue their celebration. On deck, two men were fighting over a pair of gold candlesticks while another pirate watched, drinking his ale from a priceless Chinese vase.

Inside his quarters, Barbossa stood among his own private treasure. While he had been generous with his crew, he always kept the best for himself. Gold and jewels spilled off shelves and onto the floor. A large priceless painting lay across a chaise, while in one corner were several more, heaped upon each other carelessly.

Barbossa himself had become shinier, too. His beard, which had once been ratty and knotted, was brushed smooth and shined with expensive oil. He wore a wig of thick, luscious brown curls. His clothes were made of the finest materials stolen money could buy, and his wooden peg leg had been replaced with one made of solid gold. He looked every bit the king of pirates as he sat in his ornate chair, eating orange candies and listening to the dulcet tones of a string quartet.

Suddenly, the door to his quarters burst open and Mullroy and Murtogg rushed in. The two former marines, who had turned their back on the navy and joined Barbossa's crew, were, as usual, the picture of incompetence. They fumbled over each other as they tried to talk to their captain.

"Sir," Mullroy began, elbowing Murtogg, "we know you said never to disturb you—"

"Or to come in without good cause—" Murtogg added.

"Or to speak without first asking ourselves if our thoughts were absolutely necessary . . ." Mullroy hesitated as Barbossa finally raised his head from the ledgers in front of him. He shot the newer pirates a stern look. Mullroy gulped. Perhaps *that* was one of those times when he should have thought a little bit harder. . . .

Barbossa seemed to agree. "Speak," he commanded, raising his gun and aiming it at them. "Quickly."

Both men took a nervous step back. Then, in a rush, they informed Barbossa that three of his ships had been attacked. "All your silver at the bottom of the sea," Mullroy explained. "A captain named Salazar left one man on each ship to tell the tale. Soon enough, he'll sink your entire fleet."

As the two men rambled on, Barbossa's eyes narrowed. So Salazar was back from the dead. That fact did not surprise him. Barbossa had outlived his own curse and learned that the seas had a way of bringing back that which had been thought lost. Nor did the fact that Salazar was going after pirate ships surprise him. In life, Salazar had been ruthless in his hatred of pirates. Then it had been he, not Barbossa, who had struck fear into the hearts of all those who sailed the seas under the Jolly Rogers of pirates big and small. No, nothing about the news surprised him. But it did anger—and worry—him. For if indeed it was Salazar out for revenge, it meant that Barbossa's current run of good luck was about to come to an end. And he wasn't particularly ready for that to happen.

He turned his gaze out through the large windows at the back of his quarters. He was going to need help. And not just any kind of help. To fight the cursed, he was going to need to find someone who knew the ways of the dark arts—black magic. Luckily, he happened to know of someone with just that particular talent.

Barbossa peered through the bars into the cell in front of him. From inside, he could hear someone chanting in a singsongy voice.

He took a deep breath. He liked having the bars between him and the sea witch held prisoner by the royal guards. However, he could not conduct his business with her on one side and him on the other. So while he knew it was not wise to arrive at the cell of the notorious sea witch Shansa *with* warning and it was downright foolish to arrive completely unannounced, Barbossa just hoped that perhaps the witch had the skill to have sensed his arrival. And that if he screamed, a guard might hear and come to his aid. . . .

Pushing the cell door open, he stepped inside. The chanting was coming from a woman standing over a steaming pot. As he watched, a rat crawled up the woman's arm and moved comfortably around her shoulders before settling in on one.

"I've been expecting you, Captain. Perhaps you'd like some tea?"

Slowly, the woman turned around. Barbossa saw that Shansa, backlit by the fire, had not lost any of her unique beauty in the time that had passed since he last saw her. She was striking, with piercing eyes and sharp cheekbones and intricate tattoos patterned across her bare head, arms, and legs. Long, powerful fingers gently stroked the rat that sat on her shoulder, and even from a distance, Barbossa could have sworn she glowed with magic.

Catching sight of several more rats coming out of the pot she had just gestured to for "tea"—which looked to be a thick, bright green substance—Barbossa shook his head. "I'll pass." Her eyes narrowed and he hastily added a "thank you." Looking past her into the shadows, Barbossa made out the skeletal remains of a man. It would do him no good to prolong the interaction. He needed to get to the reason for his visit. "You and I made our deal long ago," he began. "I saved you from the gallows—"

"And I, in turn, cursed your enemies," the sea witch finished. "But now you come to me in fear, as the dead have taken command of the sea."

Barbossa nodded. That much he knew. "What be the dead wanting with me?" he asked, getting to what he *didn't* know.

Shansa turned back to her pot and looked into it. "Not you, Captain," she finally said, correcting him, seeing something in the pot that Barbossa could not. "They're searching for a Sparrow."

"Jack?" Barbossa clarified. Shansa nodded. Barbossa held back a groan. He should have known. Of course Jack would be involved in this. Somehow the wily pirate always ended up in some sort of magical misfortune. Bad luck followed him like a puppy followed bacon.

Still staring into the pot, Shansa went on. "Jack will sail for the Trident with a girl—and a Pearl."

"The Trident will never be found!" Barbossa shouted, the noise startling the rat on Shansa's shoulder. Ignoring the rodent's hiss of disapproval, Barbossa pressed on. He didn't care about Jack. He didn't care about a mythical item he knew was just that—a myth.

Shansa motioned to the pot. Barbossa moved closer. Through the steam, he watched as a scene unfolded. A large dark ship, its sails torn and its sides rotten, prowled after a helpless pirate ship. The *Silent Mary* fell upon the other ship. In moments, its dead crew had swarmed the other boat like ants over a picnic. He couldn't hear them, but Barbossa could imagine the shrill screams as the living were overtaken by the dead.

He pulled back, his face ashen beneath his beard.

"The dead are conquering the sea," Shansa said softly. "But they are unable to step on dry land. You must take to the hills."

"You mean grass?" Barbossa said, spitting out the word. "You expect me to start a farm . . . milk things . . . make cheese while they destroy all that is mine? While they sink my treasure?"

The sea witch shrugged. "Ask yourself this, Captain: is it a treasure worth dying for?"

Barbossa didn't hesitate. "Aye," he answered with a firm nod. "I'm a pirate. Always will be. How do I save what be mine?"

Shansa reached into her pocket and pulled something out. She clutched it in her hand for a moment as if weighing whether to show Barbossa the item. Finally, she uncurled her fingers. Barbossa's eyes grew wide with surprise. Shansa held Jack's beloved compass. Dropping it, she let the item swing slowly from its chain. "Jack held a compass which points you to the thing you desire most. But betray that compass . . . and it releases your greatest fear."

"And every pirate's greatest fear is Salazar!" Barbossa exclaimed. He reached out, his fingers aching to close around the compass. "How did you get this?"

"I have my ways," the sea witch replied mysteriously. "Lead them to Jack before he finds the Trident and all your treasure will come back to you."

Slowly, Barbossa reached out and took the compass from Shansa. In exchange, he gave her a small black bag. Emptying some golden coins into her hand, Shansa nodded. Their deal was done.

But he still had another deal to make. A deal with the dead.

"The sun is up! Time to die, pirate!"

The door to Jack's cell was thrown open. Two soldiers stalked over, grabbed Jack by the arms, and dragged him out into the hall. Jack hung limply, oddly calm despite the fact that, according to one of the two men, he was about to die.

As they made their way closer to the prison's exit, Jack heard someone singing. The tune was familiar, as was the voice singing it. "Dad?" Jack asked, hopeful. The last time he had seen Teague, the man had been warning him about searching for the Fountain of Youth. As Keeper of the Pirate Code, a title the usually unserious pirate took very seriously, Teague knew more than anyone about the ins and outs of the sea. It would have been a lucky twist of fate in a very unlucky moment for Jack to run into him. But as Jack passed the cell from which the singing emanated, he saw it was not his father. "Uncle Jack?" Jack cried in recognition.

"Jackie boy!" the man in the cell replied happily. He stepped forward. In the dim light of the prison, Jack saw his uncle. The man's hair was dreadlocked like Jack's own and his eyes were the same brown, although they were cloudy with age and the skin around them was wrinkled. "How's it going?" the older pirate asked his nephew.

"Can't complain, really," Jack replied, as though they were having the conversation in the pub, not a prison. "You?"

"Never better," Uncle Jack replied. "Been waiting all morning to be beaten." He paused, then leaned forward and whispered, "They have terrible service here."

"Shameful," Jack replied.

Looking around, Uncle Jack hesitated and then gestured for Jack to get closer. Jack leaned in as far as he could under the grip of the guards. "The oceans have turned to blood, Jack. Best to stay on dry land, where it's safe."

Jack Sparrow frowned. "I'm about to be executed on dry land. . . ."

"Good point," Uncle Jack acknowledged. Then he shrugged. "Have I ever told you the one about the skeleton?"

Jack sighed. His uncle had told him the joke, many times. It wasn't even that funny. "Well, it was lovely to see you . . ." He paused, struggling for the right thing to say to a relative in a prison cell. "Anyway, I hope you have a wonderful execution."

"And you as well," Uncle Jack replied. "If you're getting disemboweled, ask for Victor. He has the softest hands."

The British soldiers gave Jack's arms a yank. While he would have enjoyed nothing more than to stay and chat with his uncle—and avoid the inevitable—it seemed the soldiers felt otherwise. They continued to drag him down the hall, out of the prison, and into the main square of Saint Martin.

A rather large crowd had gathered for the "entertainment." Men, women, and children filled the square to near bursting. They shouted and jeered at the line of prisoners awaiting their deaths. Jack glanced around and saw the girl from the map shop in a cage along with several other "witches." He gave her a brief nod.

"How would you like to die, pirate?"

Jack looked up. A large guard was standing in front of him. How would he like to die? What a novel question. He had never given it much thought. There were just so many options. . . .

"Hanging, firing squad, or a new invention—the guillotine?" the guard asked, pressing him.

Jack hesitated. "Guillotine," he finally said. "Sounds French. I love the French. They invented mayonnaise. How bad can it be?"

The guard turned Jack around so that he was facing the guillotine. Jack gulped. Apparently, he did not like *all* things French. The contraption in front of him was something out of his worst nightmares. A large blade hung suspended between two wooden arms. Below it was a block with a human-neck-sized notch taken out of it. Jack gulped again. He had changed his mind. The firing squad would be lovely. Especially if he could have a blindfold . . .

"Bring the basket!"

It was too late. As Jack protested, he was shoved down on the block. His head hung over the basket while his hands were strapped down. "Here's an idea," Jack said, his words a bit muffled due to his head's position on the chopping block. "Why don't we try a good old-fashioned stoning? Gets the crowd involved."

Across from where Jack was facing his fate, Carina Smyth was facing hers, as well. A noose had been placed around her neck and she had been led to the gallows. She stood on the tall wooden platform, looking out at the crowd. "Good sirs," she said, trying even then to make the people of Saint Martin see reason, "I'm not a witch. But I forgive your common dim-wittedness and feeble brains. In short, most of you have the mind of a goat—"

"Is it not common practice for those being executed to be offered a last meal?"

Jack's shout interrupted Carina mid-protest. She

glared across the square at the pirate. "I believe I was making a point. If you could just be patient . . ." She had not been acquainted with this Jack Sparrow character for long, but it had been long enough for her to know that it seemed always to be about him—a trait he was proving with every passing moment.

"My head is about to be lopped off—hence the emergency," he called.

"And my neck is to be broken," Carina pointed out.

"On occasion the neck doesn't break," Jack retorted. "I've seen men swing for hours, the life slowly choking out of them. The point is it's entirely possible you still have hours left to whisper your last words, whereas my head will soon be in this basket, staring up at my lifeless body—which happens to be famished!"

"Kill the filthy pirate. I'll wait," Carina announced dryly.

From his spot on the block, Jack lifted his hands and tried to shake his head. "I wouldn't hear of it," he said, feigning gallantry. Then he smirked. "Witches first."

Carina let out a scream of frustration. "I am not a witch! Were you not listening?"

"Hard to listen with the mind of a goat!" Jack shot back.

"Enough!"

Lieutenant Scarfield's voice echoed over the square, silencing the bickering pair. "Kill them both!" he ordered.

Raising his eyes as far as he could, Jack saw the executioner step forward. He wore the black mask that was required of his job. Jack watched the man's thick black gloves reach out, ready to hit the switch that would bring down the blade.

Jack closed his eyes and waited for the sound of the blade dropping.

But that sound never came. Instead, there was a whoosh and then a shout. Opening one eye, Jack saw young Henry Turner standing in the middle of the square. He was hopelessly surrounded by soldiers but still had his fists raised. A rope—presumably what

Henry had used to swing in on—hung off his wrist. Clearly the boy had attempted a rescue maneuver—and failed.

"Get another noose!" Scarfield ordered from the stands. "He will die with the others." He turned and shouted at Henry with a snarl, "Did you think you could defeat us, boy?"

Henry shook his head. "No, sir," he replied, letting a smile creep across his face. "I'm just the diversion." He turned and shouted over his shoulder, *"Fire!"*

Instantly, an explosion rocked the square. Rock and debris flew through the air and chaos erupted as people began screaming and running. The guillotine toppled over, spinning around and around as though on an axle before finally settling upside down, leaving Jack dangling helplessly from the contraption.

Scarfield's face grew red as he watched Jack's old crew lead a cannon farther into the square. He turned and saw that Henry had broken free from the soldiers holding him in the chaos. Scarfield had been tricked—by a mere child! Turning back to his men, he gave them the order to attack. But it was no use. As he watched, the pirates continued to swarm the square.

The cannon fired again, sending a group of horses scattering. They raced forward, running right at the guillotine. Seeing them moving toward him, Jack struggled to get out of the way, but there was nowhere for him to go. Once again, he closed his eyes, waiting for his inevitable death, this time at the hands—or rather, hooves—of the horses. And once again, the moment never came. Instead, the horses slammed into the side of the guillotine, sending it crashing to its other side. With a groan, the wood broke, setting Jack free. He sat up and rubbed his wrists. That had been close.

Just then the blade fell—landing right between Jack's legs.

Yikes. That had been even closer.

Getting to his feet, Jack brushed off his jacket and

wiped off his newly reacquired pants. "Gibbs!" he said, spotting his first mate. "I knew you'd come crawling back."

The bearded man shrugged. "The Turner boy paid us ten pieces of silver to save your neck," he explained.

Jack shrugged. Fair enough. Turning, he looked across the square. His freedom, while most important, was only part of the plan. He hated to admit it, and he wouldn't—not out loud, at least—but he wasn't the person they truly needed to find the Trident. They needed Henry's witch.

The only problem was she was still attached to the gallows.

As soldiers tried to fight their way through the surging crowd all around her, Carina stood helpless. She saw Henry in the middle of a group of men, punching and kicking his way toward her. A soldier suddenly appeared on the platform next to her. Carina was straining against the ropes around her wrists when a scruffy pirate with a glass eye rushed up and started fighting the soldier, sending him right off the platform.

"Thank you," Carina said, surprised.

"M'lady." The pirate extended his arms and bowed. Unfortunately, he hit the gallows switch with his hand, and Carina's stomach—and body—dropped straight down. The floor beneath her feet had opened, and the rope around her neck pulled tauter and tauter.

Her scream died in her throat as her descent came to a sudden stop. Looking down, she saw that Henry was standing underneath the platform. His arms were wrapped around her, his face buried in her stomach. She could see him struggling to keep her from falling any farther.

"From this moment on," he said, his voice muffled, "we are to be allies."

"Considering where your left hand is, I'd say we are more than that," she shot back, trying to hold her body steady.

"We find the Trident together," Henry said, not addressing Carina's ill-timed teasing. "Do I have your word?"

She nodded. Then, realizing that he couldn't see her response from his rather scandalous position, she added, "You're holding everything *but* my word. Now cut me down!"

There was a pause. "I don't have a sword at the moment."

Carina's eyebrows shot up. He didn't have a sword? What kind of soldier arrived at a rescue with nothing but his two fists? She was dangling at the end of a hangman's noose with a young man she barely knew cradling her in some overly familiar places while pirates and soldiers fought all around her. It couldn't possibly get any worse.

"Well, look at this."

Carina grimaced. Apparently it *could* get worse. Looking up, she watched Lieutenant Scarfield stalk toward Henry beneath her.

"If I kill the coward, the witch hangs," he observed. "Two for the price of one."

"Don't let go," Carina told Henry.

Henry gulped. "It'll be difficult once he kills me." With Carina in his arms, Henry was defenseless. His midsection was completely exposed. It would take nothing but a well-placed stabbing to end his life and then Carina's. He tried to think of a plan as Scarfield drew back his sword. The man's face filled with murderous glee, and then Scarfield dropped to the ground.

Behind his prone body stood Jack Sparrow. In his hand he held the dull end of the guillotine blade. "Gentlemen," he said over his shoulder to his gathered crew, "these two prisoners will lead us to the Trident."

"Prisoners?" Henry said as he was grabbed roughly by a pirate. "I convinced your men to save you! Paid them with my own silver! We had a deal!"

"There's been a slight modification." Jack shrugged as he turned and began to walk out of the square. Henry really *was* like his father—naive and silly. But while he was both those things, he was also a key to getting away from Salazar and finding the Trident. So like it or not, Jack was taking him—and his witchy little friend—along for *his* adventure.

Chapter Eight

The seas were angry. Heavy waves pounded the side of the *Queen Anne's Revenge* as it sailed under a dark gray sky. On the horizon, massive storm clouds had formed, turning everything dark.

Everything including the *Silent Mary*.

Captain Salazar's ghost ship sailed through the stormy seas, untouched by the heavy waves. The storm seemed to follow the ship as though somehow controlled by it.

Aboard the *Revenge,* Barbossa stood at the wheel, his eyes—clouded over like the seas themselves—determined and cold, fixed on the ship ahead. He knew his crew thought he had lost his mind. No one sailed *toward* the *Silent Mary*. It was a death sentence to do so, yet Barbossa had made his orders clear. They were not to stop until they were nigh on top of the other ship.

The distance between the two ships became smaller and smaller. Across from each other, the captains locked eyes, each daring the other to back down. Neither took the dare. As the *Revenge* got closer to the *Mary*, the ghost ship seemed to rise out of the water. Its skeletal hull appeared to open like the mouth of a giant beast, the wooden ribs of its bottom like teeth eager to snap the *Revenge* in half.

Calmly, Barbossa walked to the railing of his ship. "Captain Salazar," he called out across the water, "I hear you're looking for Jack Sparrow."

The ship stopped, inches from the *Queen Anne's Revenge*. There was a long, tense moment as the crew of the *Revenge* waited. And then Captain Salazar and his ghostly crew jumped down onto the *Revenge*, pulling weapons as they landed silently on the decks. Landing in front of his men, Captain Salazar stalked over to

Barbossa, who couldn't help staring at the gaping hole in Salazar's skull. Barbossa swallowed hard.

"It's impolite to stare," Captain Salazar said in greeting. "Have you never seen a fatal wound before?"

Barbossa averted his eyes from the hole. "My name is Captain Barbossa," he began. "And I stand before you with cordial intent."

Pulling out his sword, Salazar began to walk around the other captain. "Cordial intent?" he repeated. He turned to his crew. "Do you hear that, men?" The ghosts laughed, the sound sending shivers down the spines of the living pirates. Looking back at Barbossa, he went on. "I am going to show you what cordial means. Every time I tap my sword, one of your men will die. So I suggest you speak quickly." To prove his point, Salazar brought his sword down on the wood. Before the sound of the tap could fade, there was a scream from the back of the deck. "Tell me where Jack is—I'm waiting." He tapped his sword on the deck menacingly.

"He's going for the Trident . . ." Barbossa said in a rush.

"The sea belongs to the dead," Salazar replied.

Barbossa inclined his head, acquiescing to the other captain. "But the Trident controls the sea. . . ."

It was the wrong thing to say. Salazar's sword rose and he closed in on Barbossa. "There is no treasure that can save him!" he shouted. "He will die! As will you!"

Barbossa raised his hands. "I be the only one who can lead you to him," he said quickly. "I declare, you'll have Jack's life before sunrise on the morrow—or you can take mine. Do we have an accord?"

For one long moment, Salazar said nothing, weighing the offer. Finally, he nodded. "Take me to him, and you will live to tell the tale."

"You have my word. I thank you on behalf of my crew."

Salazar smiled. Then, very slowly, he tapped his sword. There was a scream and Barbossa flinched. Then Salazar tapped the sword again. And again. And two more times after that. With each tap, there was a horrible cry and Barbossa's crew became one man smaller. "You can take what's left of them," Salazar said cruelly. Then he turned and gave his orders. "The living come aboard."

As a plank was dropped between the two ships, Barbossa turned and signaled to his men. He had made his deal and had to see it through, even if it meant stepping onto a ghost ship and putting his life—and the lives of his crew—in the hands of a mad pirate-hating ghost. Not for the first time, he uttered a silent curse against Jack Sparrow. Somehow, the wily pirate always seemed to be getting him into trouble. This time, though, it would be he, Captain Hector Barbossa, getting *Jack* into hot water.

Henry Turner had done his fair share of daydreaming about being caught up in an adventure with a beautiful girl. He had not, however, dreamed that the adventure would include being tied to the mast of a dingy ship belonging to a rather crazy captain and manned by his delinquent crew. Yet that was *exactly* where this adventure had landed him. He now found himself tied, rather too tightly in his opinion, to the mast of the *Dying Gull*. On the other side of the mast, Carina Smyth struggled against her restraints, muttering under her breath.

"Carina," Henry said as he stared nervously out at the sea. On the horizon, he could see the coming storm and knew what it meant. "There's something you need to know. The dead are sailing straight for us."

On her side of the mast, Carina raised an eyebrow. "Is that so?" she asked, smirking.

"Yes," Henry replied sincerely. "I've spoken to them."

"Have you spoken to krakens and mermaids as well?" she teased.

Henry, unaware the girl was mocking him, replied in earnest. "Krakens don't speak. Everyone knows that."

Carina sighed at the foolish boy and his foolish beliefs. It was clear he was not right in the head. Plus, it was he who had led her straight into that mess of being tied up on a pirate ship in the first place. "I never should have saved you."

Realizing it would do no good to retort, Henry decided to start talking about the task at hand, attempting to turn his head toward her. "Last night there was a blood moon, just as you described. Tell me what it revealed."

"And why should I trust you?" she asked.

"You trusted me to hold your port, remember," Henry said, surprised by his own boldness. The flirty words had left his mouth before he could stop them. He heard Carina's shocked intake of breath and her protest. He smiled. Since meeting Carina, he had always felt at a loss for words. But now she was the one struggling to find the right thing to say. "Tell me what you found," Henry went on. "And I promise to help you."

He felt the ropes tighten around his chest as Carina adjusted herself on the other side of the mast. For a long moment, she did not speak. Henry wished he could see her face to try to glean some idea of what she was thinking. Had he pushed it too far with his teasing? Was she just not going to speak again . . . ever? Finally, he heard her mumble something under her breath.

"I've been alone my entire life," she said. "I don't need any help."

Henry shook his head. He didn't believe that. At least not all of it. "Then why did you come to me, Carina?" he asked, pushing her. "Why are we tied together in the middle of the sea chasing the same treasure? Maybe you can't see it—but our destiny is undeniable."

"I don't believe in destiny," Carina replied bluntly.

"Then believe in me," Henry said, the teasing tone completely gone from his voice. He was serious as he added, "As I believe in you."

There was another long pause, and once again, Henry feared he had gone too far. But finally, she sighed. "The moon revealed a clue, Henry," she said. "'To release the power of the sea, all must divide.'"

"What does it mean?" Henry asked, confused.

To his surprise, Carina did not have an answer at the ready. In fact, she admitted, albeit grudgingly, that she didn't know what the convoluted clue meant.

"Then we'll just have to find out," Henry said, not willing to give up on his dream of finding the Trident.

"There is no map in this map." Jack's voice instantly reminded Henry that, unfortunately, he and Carina weren't the only ones on that journey. Nor were they in a particularly good spot to do any finding of any sort. Looking up, he saw the captain swaying over. Jack was holding the diary of Galileo in his hand. He held it up in front of Carina, who tried in vain to reach for it. "Give me the Map No Man Can Read."

"If you could read it," Carina said testily, "then it wouldn't be called the Map No *Man* Can Read."

Jack shrugged. "Most of the men on this ship can't read. So . . . that makes all maps the Map No Man Can Read."

Henry groaned. Jack was a fool to try to argue with Carina. Henry didn't know her well—or at all, really—but he knew she would not just give in. Not without a well-orated debate, at least. He was right.

"If no one can read it," Carina pointed out, "then you have no use for it or me."

Jack raised a hand to his goatee and twirled the knotty hair in his fingers. Then he held out his other hand and began moving the fingers as though doing some sort of intense calculation. Coming to a conclusion, he shrugged. "Let me start again. Show. Me. The. Map!"

"I. Can't."

Carina's snippy response made Henry cringe.

"It does not yet exist," she went on.

There were murmurs from the crew, who had gathered around the mast. "She's a witch!" Marty said, voicing aloud what everyone was saying quietly.

"No," Carina said, shooting the small pirate a huge glare, "I'm an astronomer."

Henry rolled his eyes. There was no way those pirates were going to know what an astronomer was.

So it was no shock to him when Scrum asked if that meant Carina bred donkeys.

The girl let out a frustrated groan. "An astronomer," she explained through her clenched jaw, "contemplates the sky." She lifted her head toward the stormy one above.

"On a donkey?" Scrum asked.

"There is no donkey!" shouted Carina.

"Then how do you breed them?" another pirate asked.

Henry stifled a laugh. He could practically feel the anger radiating from Carina. While he couldn't see her face, he could almost guarantee that a scowl marked her beautiful features. He had not spent much time with pirates, but he had heard enough stories to be prepared for their illogical thinking—or lack of thinking entirely. Carina, on the other hand, clearly had anticipated finding the map with a few more men of intelligence.

Growing tired of his crew's line of questioning and fancying himself a bit brighter than his counterparts,

Jack stepped up to Carina. "Allow me to simplify this equation," he said. "Give me the map, or I'll kill him." He drew his gun and aimed it at Henry.

"Go ahead and kill him," Carina said nonchalantly. "You're bluffing."

Jack raised an eyebrow. "And you're blushing." Sure enough, Carina's face had turned a becoming shade of pink. He looked to his men. "Throw him over!"

Several of the pirates immediately untied Henry from the mast. Grabbing him by the arms, they walked him over to the rail of the ship. Then they tied a long rope to his hands.

"He doesn't appear to be bluffing!" Henry shouted over his shoulder.

Jack nodded. "We call this keelhauling," he explained. "Young Henry will be tossed over and dragged under the ship." He waited for Carina's response.

If he had been expecting begging of some sort, Jack was sadly mistaken. Carina simply shrugged. "Go on," she said. "What are you waiting for?"

As Carina watched, the men gagged Henry and unceremoniously tossed him overboard. Carina stifled a cry. She pulled her gaze back to Jack and met his eyes. She tried not to flinch and stayed still as the captain peered over the rail and informed her that Henry was not a very strong swimmer. She even managed not to show any emotion when Gibbs pointed out that Henry would be lucky to drown before the barnacles sliced him open. But when Jack mused that the blood would inevitably attract sharks, Carina finally could no longer stand it. "We're wasting time!" she said, trying to sound calm despite the panic flooding through her. "Bring him up!"

"All of him?" Jack asked. "Because that might be a problem in a few moments."

"The map is there!" Lifting her arm as far as she could, she pointed up to the sky.

"On your finger?" Marty asked after a beat.

Carina held back her scream of frustration. "It's in the heavens!" she said, not including the "you dimwit" she so badly wanted to add. "That diary will lead me to a map *hidden in the stars.*"

Jack walked back to Carina. He leaned forward so his face was mere inches from hers and stared, trying to decide if she was bluffing. "A treasure map written in the stars?" he repeated, to be sure.

She nodded. "Bring him up and I will find it tonight!"

"Sorry," Jack said after a lengthy pause, during which Carina had to feel his rum-scented breath on her face. Then he untied her. "Can't bring him up. Look for yourself."

Rushing to the side of the boat, Carina braced herself for the worst. She expected to see blood. Or body parts. Or both. But to her surprise, she saw a very alive, very unbloody, and all-in-one-piece Henry Turner, albeit still bound and gagged. He was staring up at her from the bow of a rowboat that floated next to the *Dying Gull*. She whirled around.

Jack was watching her, a wry expression on his face. "As I said . . . blushing."

Carina's nostrils flared and her blue eyes narrowed. "You're confused," she said, trying to calm her racing heart and hoping against hope Jack couldn't see the pulse speeding in her neck. "I am here for one reason."

"I know how this works," Jack said. "The stolen glances, beads of sweat on the brow, drips of sweat behind the neck . . ."

"That boy is nothing to me," Carina said, involuntarily checking the back of her neck. "Now give me the diary and stay out of my way!" She snatched the diary from Jack and stalked off.

Behind her, Jack smiled. "The scent of desire does not lie." Then he paused and raised his arm. He took a big sniff. "Although, that could be me. . . ."

Chapter Nine

Night had finally fallen over the Caribbean Sea. Carina stood at the bow of the *Dying Gull,* her long dark hair blowing gently around her face. Reaching up, she absently pushed a strand out of her eyes, unaware of her beauty in the moonlight.

It had taken her so long to get to that moment. Years of study. Thousands of pages read by candlelight. Endless torment and mockery by dozens who couldn't fathom a girl's wanting to learn things such as astronomy and cartography. And while she'd figured out that more information could be found during a blood moon, she still didn't know exactly how to find the map.

She sighed, turning the worn diary over. It had been left to her by the father she had never met, a father who had clearly intended for her to study the stars. A wave of sadness washed over her. Normally she was able to keep it at bay. It had done her no good to be melancholy—not at the orphanage where she had grown up, not in the handful of places she had called home since then. But every once in a while, the thought of what her life *could* have been crept up and overwhelmed her. What would it have been like if she hadn't been left at the children's home as a baby? Would she be standing at the bow of some other ship, staring up at the heavens with her father?

Carina shook her head. It was not the time to get lost in what-ifs and maybes. She had work to do. Glancing over her shoulder, she saw Henry watching her from across the deck. His handsome face was unreadable in the moonlight, and she couldn't help wondering what he was thinking—if he was wondering about his own father, the one he believed to be cursed by the sea.

Henry was not, in fact, thinking of his father at that moment. He was preoccupied by the flashes of lightning in the distance. They were too patterned to be natural, which could mean only one thing. . . .

Making his way across the deck, he found Jack Sparrow asleep, a bottle of rum held loosely in his hand. Henry nudged him. The man gave a snort but did not wake. He nudged him again, harder. Still, Jack didn't wake. Looking around, Henry saw a bucket of dirty water left behind by a crew member who had been on cleaning duty. Henry picked it up—and then dumped it over Jack.

The pirate woke. With a shout, he leapt to his feet. "What are you doing?" he asked, shaking the water off him as though it were poison. "It's not my week to bathe!"

"Look out to sea," Henry said, pointing to the lightning. "Salazar is out there!"

Jack's gaze followed Henry's finger. Then he looked back at the young man and arched an eyebrow. "You woke me for that?" He took a long swig from his bottle and went to lie back down.

Henry stifled a groan. He was beginning to understand why his father had told him to stay away from Jack Sparrow. From what he could tell, the pirate was nothing but a drunk with a predisposition for rum and an uncanny ability to do a whole lot of nothing and have it benefit him. "The dead are hunting us down and you do nothing!" he finally shouted, not able to hide his frustration any longer.

"Nothing?" Jack repeated. "You call this nothing?"

"You're drunk and sleeping," Henry pointed out.

Jack nodded proudly. "Exactly. I'm doing two things at once."

Henry had had enough. He needed to get through to Jack somehow, and talking did not seem to be working. He grabbed a sword that had been left on deck, lifted it up, and tried to hold it to Jack's chest. It shook in his hands, the steel heavier than he had anticipated. "Like it or not," he said, trying to sound as threatening as possible, "you're going to help me, Jack. I *will* break my father's curse!"

Expecting a pithy remark, Henry was surprised when, instead, Jack reached out and adjusted his fingers on the sword. "Lighten your grip," he advised, turning Henry's hand slightly. "Square the pommel. Front leg bent." He waited for Henry to bend his right leg slightly. Then he nodded. "Much better. Now, run me through."

"What?" Henry said, startled.

Jack nodded again. "One quick strike should kill me," he said. "Or if you'd like, I could get a running start and hop onto the blade."

Henry scowled. "Maybe I'm not a pirate," he said, lifting his sword higher and staring straight into Jack's eyes, "but you're wrong if you think I wouldn't do it."

In response, Henry heard the cocking of a gun. Lowering his gaze, he saw that Jack was now holding his pistol. It was aimed up at Henry's head. "And *you're* wrong if you think I'd let you. Next time you raise a sword, be the last to die."

Henry opened his mouth to point out the lack of

logic in Jack's statement, but at that moment, Carina walked by. She didn't even bother to give the two men a glance. Instead, she remained focused on the diary in her hand. Henry's eyes followed her for a moment before snapping back to Jack. To his annoyance, the pirate was watching him watch Carina with an amused expression on his face.

"I suggest you entice her with flattery," Jack said. "You can start with what I always say: 'Would you mind washing that?' "

"I'm *not* interested in Carina!" Henry insisted.

Jack clapped his hands together, his rings clinking. "I knew it! She's all you think of!" He leaned closer to Henry, the gun and sword forgotten, and whispered conspiratorially, "A bit of discretion when courting a redhead—never pursue her sister. But, if you cannot avoid the charms of her sister—kill her brother." Henry raised an eyebrow. He didn't want to know how Jack knew so much about something so scandalous. The pirate went on, clearly enjoying himself. "And if she attempts to give you a piece of salted meat, assume it's poisoned. Unless she's a twin—in which case, still kill the brother. Savvy?"

Henry's head was spinning. "No!" he shouted. "I do not savvy!"

"Well, that wisdom will cost you five pieces," Jack said.

"I'm not paying you for that," Henry countered.

Jack smiled and laid a hand on Henry's shoulder. "Never say that to a woman," he advised. "They get very upset." Then, whistling to himself, he turned and swayed back to his spot on the deck, plopped down, took one long swig of rum, and promptly fell asleep.

Looking down at him, Henry groaned. If Jack Sparrow was really the key to saving his father, Henry was in a lot of trouble.

The moon had risen still higher in the night sky as Henry stood on the deck of the *Dying Gull*. A spyglass was raised to his eye as he scanned the horizon. Hearing footfalls, he lowered the spyglass. Carina had come over and was standing next to him.

"What are you doing?" she asked softly.

Henry hesitated. There was something very intimate about speaking under the stars to a beautiful woman. His heartbeat quickened ever so slightly as he met Carina's warm and questioning gaze. Her blue eyes were bright, even in the darkness of night.

"Looking for him," Henry finally said. "Even when I know he's not there." As soon as the words left his mouth, Henry wished he could take them back. He sounded like a little boy, not the man he hoped Carina saw him as.

To his surprise, she didn't laugh at him. Instead, her eyes grew sad. "Just because you can't see something doesn't mean it's not there."

"Like the map?" Henry guessed.

She nodded. "I have to find it," she said, her voice determined.

"No one has ever found it," Henry pointed out. "Maybe it doesn't exist."

Carina's head whipped around as though Henry had hit her, not just said what he assumed many other people had already said to her over the years. She held up the diary and waved it in his face. "This is the only truth I know. I kept it with me each day in that orphanage, studied the heavens when it was forbidden. I swore to know the sky as my father intended me to!" Her voice cracked with emotion and she lowered her eyes. "My mother died as I was born. This diary was all that was left with me."

Her words hit Henry like a punch to the gut. They were far more similar than he had ever imagined: both forced to grow up without fathers; both on a journey to somehow right that wrong; both determined never to stop looking for the one thing that might make them feel whole. "Carina," he said, his voice gentle. She raised her eyes and met his gaze. "You're always looking to the sky. Perhaps the answer is right here."

For one long moment, Carina thought Henry meant *he* was her answer. She felt an odd pounding in her chest, and her cheeks flushed involuntarily. She was about to open her mouth to say she thought she might feel the same way, but was saved the embarrassment when he pointed to the diary. He hadn't been talking about himself. He had been talking about what was on the pages of Galileo's book! Regaining her composure, she opened the book. "Galileo wrote that 'all truths will be understood once the stars align,'" she read.

"If stars do not move, how can they align?" Henry asked, confused.

"He could be referring to the planets," Carina suggested. She pointed to a few lines on the page. "He wrote the word *derectus*. So the stars must align," she translated.

Henry leaned forward so he could see the page better. Sure enough, there, written in faded ink, was the word *derectus*. But as he stared at the word, something occurred to him. This was a language that had popped up occasionally in his studies about pirate mythology over the years. "Carina," he said, growing excited, "Galileo was Italian. But the word *derectus* is not Italian. It's Latin."

"Latin?"

Henry nodded. "And *derectus* does not mean *align*. It means *a straight line*."

Slowly, Henry's words sank in. Carina's eyes grew wide. She looked back down at the book in her hands and then up at the sky. "'All truths will be understood once the stars are in a *straight line*,'" she whispered, her mind whirling with the possibilities this new translation brought. Her finger gently rubbed the ruby on the diary's cover. Then she gasped. The answer had been right in front of her the whole time. "There is a straight line moving from Orion—the son of Poseidon!"

"How do you follow it?" Henry asked, his excited tone echoing Carina's.

"The line begins with the ruby. A straight line from the ruby . . ." Her voice trailed off as she moved to free the gem from its cover. Holding it up to the sky, she peered through it like a lens in a spyglass. Henry went to her and stood beside her so that he, too, could look through the stone.

"Do you see that?" Henry asked, gasping as he spotted a red line that burned across the sky.

Carina nodded. "A straight line starting in Orion—the hunter's arrow moving straight through Cassiopeia—heading across the sky toward the end of the Southern Cross! It ends there!"

"So the map is *inside* the cross?" Henry asked, trying to follow Carina's line of thinking and failing.

"No," she said, shaking her head. "Because it's not a cross! It's an X! The Southern Cross is an X hidden in the sky since the beginning of time! *This* is the Map No Man Can Read!" She grabbed Henry's hand excitedly.

"That map will lead us to the Trident!" Henry said, beginning to bounce excitedly on his toes. "We just have to follow the X!"

The pair's jubilation was rudely brought to an abrupt halt by the sound of a dozen guns cocking. Slowly, Henry and Carina turned around.

Standing there, having overheard the majority of their discovery, were Jack and his motley crew. The pirate captain was smiling. Once again, his plans had gone swimmingly; he had done nothing and yet gotten everything he needed. Now he knew just where he was going. X, after all, always marked the spot!

Chapter Ten

Barbossa was no stranger to the strange. After all, he had, at one time, been cursed to take skeletal form in the moonlight. Yet even that unfortunate period had not prepared him for being aboard the *Silent Mary* with its ghostly crew.

Since boarding the *Silent Mary,* Barbossa and his men had been witness to the futility of the ghost crew's life. Not only were they cursed to live after death, stuck on a ship with various forms of wounds that would never heal; they were cursed to crew for Captain Salazar. And he was a ruthless captain—as much in death as he had been in life. The mood on the ship was always as dark as its rotten sides.

Standing at the ship's helm, Barbossa watched as the ghosts scrubbed the blood-soaked deck, even though no matter how hard they scrubbed, the blood remained. Still, Salazar shouted his orders. "Scrub that deck! The *Silent Mary* will be the pride of the Spanish fleet!" Turning, Salazar made his way to Barbossa. "Your time is up," he said.

Barbossa carefully felt for Jack's compass in his pocket. He had kept it, his ticket off the ship, hidden. He couldn't afford to lose it or, worse, have it taken. Then he cleared his throat. "Not to disagree," he said diplomatically, "but our accord spoke of the sunrise. That be first light—far from a risin' sun. And you bein' a man of honor—" His words caught in his throat as Salazar raised his sword to his neck. He gulped. "My own death I can live with, Captain," he finally said. "But what will haunt me is not knowing the cause of my demise. Surely you would grant me a simple tale as we await the light—to know what Jack Sparrow did to bedevil the dead?"

The sword in Salazar's hand did not lower. "The dead man's tale is never to be told!" he said with a sneer.

Barbossa nodded. "Aye," he said in agreement.

"Unless spoken *to* the dead—which I am presently to be." He waited, hoping his reasoning would not be lost on the ghost captain. The sword lowered a fraction. Taking that as a good sign, Barbossa forged on. "Now I heard stories of a Spanish captain—*El Matador del Mar.* A man who scourged the sea without equal—who hunted and killed thousands of men—"

"Not men," Salazar said, correcting him. "Pirates!" Then, ever so slowly, he brought his sword down. Turning from Barbossa, he looked over his crew of dead degenerates. It had been ages since he had been known as *El Matador del Mar.* Ages since he had been able to do the one thing that brought him happiness: destroy pirates. And the only reason he had been stopped, the only reason he was now stuck there, like that, was Jack Sparrow.

Still looking at his crew, Salazar began to tell his tale. His voice was low, and if Barbossa had believed ghosts capable of having souls, he would have sworn the man sounded wistful as he spoke. The *Silent Mary,*

Salazar pointed out, had not always looked the way it did now. At one point, it had been the pride of the Spanish Navy, and he, as the ship's captain, a hero. The ship had more weapons than five ships combined. Its many levels of decks were always spotless, as were the uniforms of the men who crewed it. Salazar commanded all this with a vicious ease. He led by example: his face kept clean-shaven, his uniform pressed every morning, his shoes polished, his sword shining.

Over the years, Salazar's reputation as a pirate hunter grew as he stalked the seas looking for the telltale Jolly Rogers. When he spotted one, the *Silent Mary* would drop all its sails and speed over the waves as though powered by some magical force. The pirate ships never stood a chance. Nor did their crews.

"I destroyed dozens of ships—until there were only a handful left," Salazar growled. "The last ones joined together to try to defeat me. But they soon realized it was hopeless. Nothing could stop my *Silent Mary*."

The pirate ships went down one by one. Survivors littered the water, illuminated by the light of their burning ships. They begged for mercy. Captain Salazar's lieutenant wondered if they should oblige.

But Salazar would not hear of it. "You know my father was an admiral—and a traitor. He patrolled these very waters, took bribes from pirates—gold and silver—allowed them to sail with impunity!" His hands shook with fury. "He was arrested when I was a boy, and soon after, they came to our house and took my mother away, dragged her to a workhouse. The wife of a traitor must pay for his sins."

Salazar's father was released from prison a year after his mother died in the spike. And when he returned, Salazar greeted him with a knife. "I gutted him like the coward he was. And that day I made a vow to myself—I would kill them all."

So there was no mercy for the helpless pirates in the water. Upon Salazar's nod, the *Silent Mary*'s crew opened fire on the water, the last of the pirate ships burning before their eyes. Salazar thought the battle was over, thought he had purified the waters once and for all.

But then he heard an unfamiliar, defiant voice cut through his victory. "Lovely day for a sail, Captain! Wouldn't you agree?"

One last ship was gliding through the smoke, attempting to escape Salazar's clutches. In the ship's crow's nest, a young pirate called to Captain Salazar without fear.

"The way I see it," the young pirate cried, "there's just the two of us left. Surrender to me now, Captain, and I will let you live."

The pirate's captain had been killed in the battle and had left him with a compass and a crew in need of leadership. The odds were stacked against him. But still the pirate mocked Salazar, jumping up and hoisting the Jolly Roger so that it waved with gusto.

"He stood there and was looking like a bird; he was like a little bird," Salazar told Barbossa now. "And from that day he earned himself a name that would haunt me for the rest of my days—*Jack the Sparrow*!"

Incensed and determined not to let such an insolent pirate live, Salazar commanded his men to follow the pirate ship through the mist. Jack Sparrow led the *Silent Mary* toward the mouth of the Devil's Triangle, instructing his crew to alter their course at the last moment. As the pirate ship made a 180-degree turn, the *Silent Mary* sailed under the looming arch, rocked by Sparrow's ship. Captain Salazar was knocked in the head and fell into the dark waters. His men rushed to his aid, not yet knowing what was in store for them.

Young Jack Sparrow and his crew sailed off into the sunset, Jack's compass pointing him toward the one thing he desired most—a pirate's life. And Captain Salazar and his men became fragments of their former selves, bound to the Devil's Triangle.

"The Sparrow took everything from me," Salazar finally finished. "Left me to rot in the filth of death—which is where the tale ends for you!" Once more, he lifted his sword to Barbossa's throat.

But Barbossa did not look worried. Instead, he pointed to the horizon, where the sun was just coming up. "I found him, as promised!" he said.

As Salazar followed the other captain's gaze, his eyes narrowed in disbelief. Barbossa had been true to his word after all. For there, on the horizon, was the *Dying Gull*. Slowly, a sneer spread across Salazar's once handsome face. He was about to catch the Sparrow. And when he did, he would clip his wings once and for all.

Chapter Eleven

"So she's saying she has the map, but only *she* can follow it?"

Gibbs's question hung in the air, unanswered. There were two things Jack disliked more than anything else—empty rum bottles and not knowing something. When the odd moment came along that he didn't have a ready answer, he was quick to make one up. In this case, though, he was having trouble with that. Carina's ramblings and mumblings about an X in the sky were confusing, and frankly, well, they were boring him.

They were not, however, boring his crew. Instead of doing the work they *should* have been doing, they were staring up at the sky.

"Do any of you see this X?" Pike asked, his neck craned back at a painful angle.

Next to him, Scrum shook his head. He had his hand to his eyes, trying to block the sun, which shone down brightly on the deck of the *Dying Gull*. "I see a bird. And a cloud. And my own hand."

"Jack," Gibbs said, turning to his captain. Like the rest of the men, he was growing anxious. They had been sailing under the hot sun for hours and seemed no closer to whatever it was they were searching for. "How are we to follow an X to a spot where no land could exist? An X which has disappeared with the sun?"

Jack's nostrils flared and his eyes narrowed. He had had enough waiting and more than enough not knowing. He swayed across the deck to where Carina stood, staring at a metal object in her hand, and grabbed her by the arm. She let out a surprised gasp as he brought his face close to hers. "For the last time," he said, "how do we find your X?"

"This chronometer," Carina said, holding up the small metal object, "keeps the exact time in London.

I'm making an altitude measurement to the Southern Cross to determine longitude. Only then will we find that spot on the sea!"

Jack cocked his head. He had seen her mouth moving but was quite sure that Carina had just spoken in gibberish.

Marty seemed to agree. "Witch!" he cried, not willing to give up on his belief that Carina practiced magic.

"So you expect to follow your X with a timepiece?" Gibbs asked, translating Carina's words into something Jack finally understood.

Carina nodded. "My calculations are precise and true." She paused as she looked down at the chronometer. "I'm not just an astronomer. I'm also a horologist."

There was a long pause as her words echoed over the deck. The men exchanged knowing looks. It was not the first time they had met one of those. There were plenty in the various Caribbean ports.

"No shame in that, dear," Jack said, patting Carina

gently on her shoulder. "We all have to earn a living!"

Carina frowned. Why would Jack feel bad for her for being a scholar of time? He must not have heard her properly. "No, I'm a horologist!"

"So was my mum," Scrum said. "Although she didn't crow about it quite as loud as you."

"Are you saying your mother was academically inclined?" Carina asked, surprised.

"More like horizontally reclined," Jack quipped.

Suddenly, Carina's face turned red as she finally realized what the crew thought *horologist* meant. "Horology is the study of *time*!" she cried.

"So nobody can find that X but you?" Jack asked.

"And the donkey?" Scrum added helpfully.

Suddenly, Henry let out a loud yell. *"Salazar!"*

Jack jumped.

"Ship to aft!"

Gibbs's cry made everyone look behind them. And while Carina was happy they had finished their ridiculous conversation, that sense of relief was short-lived.

Because coming up on them, more swiftly than was natural, was the *Silent Mary*.

"Jack," Henry said, eyeing the ship, "the dead will not rest until they have their revenge."

All eyes turned to Jack. The dead had never been a part of the deal. As the *Silent Mary* gained on them, they began to rumble their discontent. It was one thing to try to steal a bank or to sail on a poor excuse for a ship. It was another thing altogether to be pursued by the most notorious pirate hunter to ever live—or, rather, ever live and then die and then come back.

"We should never have followed a luckless pirate and witch to sea!" Pike shouted, voicing what the rest of the crew was thinking. He pulled out his sword, and the rest of the crew followed suit.

Turning, Jack found himself surrounded by his own crew. Beside him, Henry and Carina shifted nervously on their feet as they spied the swords and guns aimed right at them.

"Kill them all!" one of the pirates cried.

Jack held up his hands. "Kill me, and the dead won't have their revenge," he pointed out.

"Which will anger them even more," Henry added.

The pirates looked confused. Some lowered their weapons slightly, clearly unsure what to do next.

Luckily, Jack had a ready answer, as he so often did. "As captain," he said, "might I suggest . . . a mutiny?"

As the rest of the crew exchanged looks, Carina rolled her eyes. She was very much looking forward to the day when she would not have to be surrounded by what seemed to be a crew of fools, led by the most foolish fool of a captain. But until that day came, she was going to have to hope that, foolish or not, Jack Sparrow truly had a plan up those dirty sleeves of his.

"Mutiny?" Carina said. "You *had* to suggest a mutiny?"

Her hopes of Jack's having a plan had turned out to be founded. Unfortunately, his plan was, in her opinion, a horrible one. A horrible plan that had started with suggesting a mutiny, continued with having the pirates carry out said mutiny, and ended with her, Jack, and Henry being set adrift in a longboat. Now she sat in the back of the boat, watching as Jack and Henry frantically rowed toward a small island. Carina cocked her head and sighed. They seemed in an awful hurry to go seemingly nowhere.

"Carina," Henry said, hearing her sigh, "they're coming."

Carina pursed her lips. She had thought better of Henry. Or at least she had thought him a bit brighter than the pirates. Yet ever since they'd been thrown from the *Dying Gull,* he had been rambling on about the dead coming for them. "Ghosts," she said, not hiding the condescending tone in her voice. "You're both afraid of ghosts."

"Yes," Jack answered. "And lizards. And Quakers."

"Well, I choose not to believe," Carina said.

Henry stopped rowing long enough to point out to sea. "Do you not see what's behind us?" he asked.

Slowly, Carina turned. Not more than a mile back, the *Silent Mary* was clearly visible. In the sky right above the ship, dark storm clouds had started to form, and the sea underneath it churned unnaturally. Quickly, Carina turned back to the two men. She crossed her arms in front of her chest. "I see a very old ship—nothing more." She hoped her voice didn't sound shaky.

As if sensing its prey's vulnerability, the *Silent Mary* suddenly picked up speed. Giant sails appeared out of nowhere, giving the ship that much more power. Seeing Jack's eyes grow wide, Carina turned around once again. The *Silent Mary* was bearing down on them and would be upon their small longboat in no time. And Carina had no intention of sticking around to see what would happen then.

Standing up, she began to unbutton her dress.

"What are you doing?" Henry said, shocked. His hands shook on the oars and he averted his eyes.

"Preparing to swim," Carina replied as though it were obvious. "Whoever those men are, they're after

Jack. And Jack is on this boat. So I'm going to swim for it."

Jack looked impressed—and annoyed. "How dare you do exactly what I would do if I were you!"

Carina continued to get undressed. "I can't very well swim in this dress!" she said when Henry told her to stop. She pulled her dress off, ignoring Jack's lecherous looks and rude comments. When she was done, she stood at the bow of the boat, covered from shoulder to ankle by her very unrevealing, unattractive underwear.

"This is by far the best mutiny I've ever had," Jack said, unbothered that Carina's undressing had not been that much of an undressing after all.

Carina shot him a look and dove into the water. She began to swim as, behind her, Henry stayed frozen in place, mortified. He had seen her ankles—both of them! It was improper and immodest and . . . well, exciting. He shook his head. Now was not the time to be distracted. And Carina *did* have a point. Captain Salazar was not after them; he was after Jack. Getting as far away from the pirate as possible was probably the best idea. He stood up and took off his own jacket.

Seeing Henry preparing to dive, Jack put a hand to his heart. "You would leave me after all I've done for you?" he asked, truly offended. "Pursue some girl in her knickers? You men are all alike!"

Henry turned and raised an eyebrow. "There's been a slight modification," he quipped. Turning back around, he prepared to dive into the water. But just as he bent his knees, a shark leapt out of the sea, missing him by mere inches!

This, however, was no ordinary shark. And it wasn't alone. A whole group of them had appeared. They moved faster than any real shark, and as Henry looked down at them circling the longboat, he saw that in places, their flesh had rotted away completely. Some were missing eyes; others had hooks still hanging from their mouths. They were ghost sharks, caught in the same Devil's Triangle curse as Salazar and his men.

And their sole intention was to kill Jack Sparrow and whoever—or whatever—got in the way.

Moving back from the edge of the longboat, Henry watched in horror as the sharks began to feed in a frenzy, taking huge chomping bites out of the wood in an effort to get to the two humans stranded inside. Henry grabbed an oar and tried to bat them away. But it was useless; his oar did not faze the beasts in the slightest. Beside him, Jack pulled out his gun and fired into the water. But that didn't work, either. The bullets disappeared into the dark, churning abyss. And the whole time, the sharks kept eating away at the boat.

"We have to swim for it!" Henry shouted. He lifted a foot just in time to avoid having it bitten off by one of the sharks. "I'll distract them!"

Henry grabbed Carina's abandoned dress from the floor of the longboat. He stuck it on one of the oars and chucked it overboard. Instantly, the sharks went after it.

At the same time, three things happened. Henry dove into the water and began to swim for shore. Jack *attempted* to dive into the water, but his foot went through a hole in the bottom of the boat, trapping him. And finally, behind them, Salazar and his men appeared, floating on *top* of the water, murder etched on their faces.

Jack looked down at his foot, then in front of him, at Henry. Then behind him, at the ghosts. He gulped. He was all about getting out of sticky situations, but that one was particularly sticky. *And particularly deadly,* he thought as a shark brushed by his foot. Flinching, Jack helplessly tried to lift his foot. But it wouldn't move. He wasn't going to get out of the boat alive. Unless . . .

His gaze landed on a grappling hook lying on the boat's floor. A small smile tugged at the corner of his lips. He had an idea.

He grabbed the hook and attached a long piece of rope to one end as the sharks grew near. As Jack watched, one of them—a very large and very holey one, in fact—started to rise right in front of the boat. Jack waited. The shark moved closer. Jack waited a little longer. The shark moved even closer. And then, just as it opened its mouth wide, Jack brought down the grappling hook and snagged the ghost shark.

Instantly, the shark took off. Holding on to the rope, Jack let the shark pull the boat through the water, steering the creature away from the ghosts and toward the island. As the boat sped past Henry, Jack reached down and grabbed the floundering boy by the collar of his shirt. Hurling him into the boat, he gave him a small nod. Henry could thank him later.

Ahead, the island grew closer and closer. Jack could see Carina pulling herself onto the shore. He tugged on the rope, and the shark turned slightly, now aimed straight for where Carina lay. "Hold on!" Jack shouted to Henry as a moment later the shark hit land and evaporated, sending the boat crashing onto the shore. Sand

and water flew into the sky, and when it cleared, Jack, Henry, and Carina lay on the beach, shaken but surprisingly unharmed.

"What is wrong with you both?" Carina asked, wiping sand from her face. Her back turned to the sea, she was blissfully unaware of the horrors happening behind her. But that was about to change.

"Carina, don't turn around," Henry warned, trying to save her from the sight.

"Let me guess," Carina said, standing up and brushing herself off. She began to pivot on her heel. "You've seen another—"

The words died in her throat as she turned around. Her body froze. At her sides, her hands began to shake. Henry's efforts had been in vain. The horror had just been revealed.

In front of them, standing like an army of the undead, was the ghostly crew of the *Silent Mary*. They floated atop the waves, unable to follow the living onto dry land. A few of them tried to move closer, but when they did, they hit an invisible border, their bodies dematerializing as they died a violent second death.

Standing slightly in front of his men, Captain Salazar stared with cold, dark eyes. "Jack the Sparrow," he said, his voice gravelly. Another wave of ghosts rushed forward only to dematerialize.

"They can't step on land!" Jack said, his expression softening. "And to think I was worried!" He began to do a little dance on the sand.

Beside him, Carina opened and closed her mouth as she struggled to comprehend the sight in front of her. She saw the men drifting through the air, *floating*, which was impossible. She saw them standing despite massive wounds in various parts of their bodies—some with entire parts of their bodies *missing*—which was also impossible. And then she heard the captain speak, which she again would have thought impossible. There really was only one explanation. And as the realization hit her, she finally found her voice. *"Ghosts!"* she screamed. "Ghosts!"

"Do you remember me, Jack?" Captain Salazar asked, ignoring Carina's cries.

Jack nodded. "You look the same. Other than that gaping hole in your skull." He peered down at the ghost's feet. Then, unable to stop himself, he asked, "Are those new boots?"

"Ghosts!" Carina's shrill voice caused Jack to jump. The girl had clearly lost it. She let out another scream and then took off running. Not hesitating, Henry followed, leaving Jack alone with his ghostly audience.

"I'll be waiting for you, Jack," Salazar went on. "You *will* know my pain."

Jack looked at Salazar, then over his shoulder at Carina and Henry. Then back at Salazar. While the reunion had been lovely, he really didn't think it needed to continue. "Love to stay and chat," he said, turning on his heel, "but my map just ran away!"

With that, Jack turned to run. Behind him, he heard Salazar let out a terrifying roar. Jack shuddered despite himself. He couldn't stay on land forever. He was a pirate, after all, meant to command a ship on the open water. And he knew that the moment he returned to the high seas, Salazar would be waiting for him.

Chapter Twelve

Lieutenant Scarfield was growing impatient. Jack, Henry, and Carina had brought shame upon his reputation when they avoided death on Saint Martin. Now he was doing everything in his power to find them—even stooping to seeking the help of the sea witch Shansa.

He watched as his men led the woman down the darkened hall of the jail, their guns drawn. They looked nervously at Shansa's slight yet commanding frame, trying to keep as much distance from her as possible. Even the other prisoners stepped back from their cells as she passed.

"You dare try and take me!" Shansa cried as all the cell doors flew open.

Scarfield remained calm. He would not let a witch shake him.

"The sea has turned to blood," he said. "Nobody can protect you anymore."

Shansa's eyes narrowed. "Who will protect you, Lieutenant?"

"The British navy. Time to serve the crown." The soldiers cocked their guns. Scarfield went on. "A soldier washed ashore talking about the Trident of Poseidon. He was looking for Jack Sparrow—the same pirate who saved a witch from the gallows."

"She is no witch." Shansa scoffed.

"But you are," Scarfield replied. "And you're going to help us. We will always command the sea."

Shansa peered at the soldier thoughtfully. "You're afraid, Lieutenant. As ships burn in the night, you want to know if you can save your own? If the Trident is real?"

Scarfield motioned to the cell behind him, to the markings on the wall the last occupant had left behind. "You're going to read that wall for me or you will die.

I want to know where Jack Sparrow is going with that witch."

Shansa moved forward, staring at Carina's equations and drawings of constellations. "Destiny is in these stars," she told Scarfield. "I will set your course."

Henry was panicking. He had lost Carina. One minute she had been plunging through the jungle in front of him, and then she had just disappeared. He had searched everywhere but found nothing—not a single trace of her.

"We have to find her," he said for the eleventh time as he and Jack made their way down a dirt road. In the distance, Henry could see a small town. He was hoping that Carina had ended up there and would be waiting for him with a scowl on her face when they arrived.

Out of the corner of his eye, Henry saw Jack raise an eyebrow. He was sashaying along as though he had not a care in the world, even while, in reality, there was a ghost captain intent on destroying him. And his only hope of truly escaping Salazar's clutches was Carina, who, as Henry had pointed out many a time since they had begun walking down the road, was missing. It infuriated Henry.

"I know what's ailing you, boy . . ." Jack said, stopping to wipe something off his pant leg. "I've seen it before in sad, half-witted idiotic dum-dums like yourself, who so stupidly find themselves out at sea, having left a beautiful, alluring young woman behind only to wind up in the arms of some strapping young bloke with perfect teeth, et cetera. . . . You've got the unscratchable itch!" He paused and scratched under his arm. "Take my word for it: time will never heal your pain. . . ."

Henry had had enough. He had listened to the pirate's ramblings for hours. He had put up with the man's crazy theories of love, and he hadn't even bothered to point out that Jack was not someone from whom he wanted to receive advice. He had even overlooked the fact that the man had gone back on his word more than once in the short time they had known each other. He had put up with it all. But enough was enough. Stopping in his tracks, he turned on Jack. "She is the only one who can find the Trident!" he said, his voice louder than he had intended. "I am *not* in love with her!"

Jack pretended to look perplexed. "Love?" he repeated. "Who said anything about love? I'm talking about scabies! Small mites that burrow under the skin. Is that not what's ailing you? It's certainly been ailing me. Has been for years—"

His excuse was cut short by a high-pitched scream coming from somewhere ahead. It was followed by "Help me!" Jack and Henry exchanged looks. That was Carina. There was no doubt. The pair took off running. They jumped off the road and pushed their way through heavy leaves and branches until they came to a clearing. Looking up, they saw Carina hanging in a net that swung slowly back and forth from a large branch.

"Help her!" Jack said to Henry.

But before the young man could act, both he and Jack were swept up into a net of their own. A moment later, a gang of rough-and-tumble men materialized from the jungle around them. Jack gulped. He recognized them. "Help . . . me?" he said just as the leader walked over and hit him on the side of the head. The last thing Jack saw before his vision went dark was the man's wicked smile. They were in trouble now. . . .

Jack woke with a start. His throat was parched and his heart was pounding. Where was he? What was he doing there? And most importantly, where was the rum?

Jack looked around and found he was surrounded by men. But they weren't just any men. They were part of Pierre "Pig" Kelly's gang. And Pig Kelly was not very fond of Jack. Glancing to his left, Jack saw Carina and Henry standing, guns aimed at their heads. Carina, he noted, was wearing a tattered red dress and holding flowers. *Odd time to change,* Jack thought just as Pig Kelly stepped forward.

"Wake up, Sparrow," the man said. His nose was smooshed nearly flat, giving him a distinctly piglike appearance. "Time to pay your debt."

"Pig Kelly," Jack said, smiling. "My old friend."

The man scowled and raised his gun. "Friend?" He turned to his men. "You hear that, boys? This lying pirate owes me a plunder of silver. But luck has brought him to Hangman's Bay—and he'll settle his debt here and now."

"Of course, Pig," Jack said, oozing false sincerity. "I've looked everywhere for you. Prayed for your safety after inadvertently paying those men to put you in a sack." He shrugged as Henry shot him an accusing look. "Name your price."

Now a devilish smile crossed the other man's face as he gestured to someone standing behind him. "Her name is Beatrice. And she's my poor widowed sister."

Jack suppressed a gasp. Pig's "poor sister" was quite

round and quite blotchy, her mouth lined with scabs and sores. When she smiled at Jack, she flashed a set of rotten yellow teeth. He grimaced.

"She's a midwife," Pig Kelly went on, clearly enjoying the moment. "Been looking for a respectable man. But they don't come to this horrid place, so you'll do."

"I'll do what?" Jack asked, not really wanting to hear the answer.

"Make an honest woman of her," Pig Kelly replied. He gave a signal, and an old man began to play a wedding march on his broken fiddle. As Jack watched with growing horror, Beatrice pulled out a veil and slipped it over her head, the thin fabric doing nothing to hide her ghastly features. Looking around, Jack finally saw that they were not in just any clearing. They were all standing under the bleached bones of a whale. They were in a seaman's chapel, which could only mean . . .

"Congratulations, Jack," Pig Kelly went on, "it's your wedding day."

Jack let out a very high-pitched scream and turned to run. But he hadn't gone two steps before he was pulled back. A rope had been tied to his neck. The other end was attached to the top of the altar. He was going nowhere.

As a priest opened his Bible and shakily took his place at the front of the altar, Pig Kelly ordered the best man and bridesmaid to be brought forward. Henry and Carina were shoved toward the altar, both struggling. *That explains the outfit,* Jack thought as the pair were positioned on either side of him. A moment later, two small children joined the wedding party.

"What are those?" Jack said, eyeing the children. They were the ugliest small humans he had ever seen.

"Our children," Beatrice said, flashing her horrible smile. Then she leaned closer to Jack and whispered in his ear, her breath smelling worse than ten dirty pirates, "Best not to look them in the eye."

Jack shuddered when the priest began. As he

ordered them to place their hands on the Bible, Jack racked his brain for any way out of the uncomfortable situation. "I have scabies!" he offered hopefully.

"So do I," Beatrice said.

"Now, say 'I do,' or I'll put a bullet in your skull," Pig Kelly ordered, ending Jack's futile attempts to avoid marriage.

"Promise me you won't miss?" Jack asked. Next to him, he heard the sound of a gun cocking as one of Pig Kelly's men aimed his gun at Henry's head. He considered his options. If he didn't go through with this sham of a wedding, Henry and Carina would be killed right along with him, which would be a shame. On the other hand, if he did go through with it, he would have to be married to Beatrice—and be a father to the two monster children—which would also be a shame.

"Wait!"

Henry's shout startled Jack. Turning, he looked expectantly at the young man. Henry's father had always had a way of getting them out of tight spots. Perhaps the trait ran in the family.

"This is not legal," Henry went on.

Jack groaned. Pig Kelly couldn't have cared less about legality. Sure enough, the bride's brother ignored Henry's protest and urged the priest to continue.

But just when it looked like Jack's days as a bachelor—or his days in general—were about to end, there was a loud bang as a gun went off. One of the ribs of the whale skeleton shattered into a thousand pieces. Raising his hands to protect himself from the falling debris, Jack slowly turned. He had recognized the sound of that particular blunderbuss.

"Ah, Jack! We meet again!"

Barbossa stood, his gun still smoking, at the edge of the makeshift altar. His golden peg leg glimmered in the sun, and a large feathered hat shaded his eyes. His men stood a few feet behind him, watching the scene unfold.

"Hector?" Jack said, genuinely perplexed by the man's sudden appearance. "Who invited you to my wedding? Did you bring me a present?"

In response, Barbossa strode closer. Lifting his gun once more, he shot Pig Kelly right in the kneecap. As the man let out a pained shriek, his gang took off running. In moments, the altar had been cleared of enemies.

"Thanks," Jack said as the other man freed him from his rope. "It's just what I've always wanted. I must say, you look marvelous." He glanced at Barbossa's fancy outfit, complete with gold buttons.

Barbossa inclined his head in thanks. "And I'm amazed how you've managed to maintain your youthful appearance."

As the two men continued to go back and forth with oddly warm greetings, Barbossa's crew member Mullroy looked back and forth, confused. That was not the reunion he had anticipated when Barbossa had agreed to go on dry land in Salazar's place, find Jack, and return him to the *Silent Mary*. In fact, that was not the reunion he would have anticipated even if that had not been the case. Last he had checked, Barbossa and Jack were, well, at odds.

"Um, Captain," he said hesitantly. "Shouldn't we be, um, getting back to Salazar so we can trade Jack's life for our own?"

Barbossa nodded, not needing a reminder of the agreement. "Aye," he said. "That we *could*—but I have come for the Trident of Poseidon!"

His announcement seemed to echo off the whale bones, bouncing to each of Barbossa's men until, one by one, they realized exactly what their captain had in mind. "You're going to double-cross the dead?" Murtogg finally said.

"But you promised!" Mullroy protested.

Barbossa shot the ex-marine a glare. How dare he question his plans? Barbossa knew exactly what he was doing. "With the Trident of Poseidon, I will gut the dead who stole my command of the sea!" he said. He added silently, *Salazar will rue the day he dared cross Hector Barbossa.*

While Barbossa laid out his revised plan to his crew, Jack listened eagerly. He had always enjoyed watching Barbossa when the man's hackles were raised. He was quite the force to be reckoned with when that happened. And although he liked the other captain's new plan—especially seeing as he would benefit quite gloriously—there were two small problems. "Firstly," he said to Barbossa, "I don't wish us to die. And secondly, no vessel can outrun that shipwreck. . . ."

"But there is one, Jack," Barbossa said, having already anticipated that problem. He drew his sword and aimed it at Jack. The pirate took a nervous step back. "And she be the fastest ship at sea. The *Pearl*"—he tapped the bottle under Jack's coat—"entrapped in that bottle by Blackbeard five winters ago."

Jack opened his mouth to point out that while he

remembered all too well what Blackbeard had done and appreciated the confidence in his ship, it would do them little good in its current state. But before he could say anything, Barbossa once again surprised him. Raising his sword high above his head, Barbossa began to swing it around in a circle.

"By the power of that blackguard's sovereign blade, I hereby release the *Black Pearl* to claim her former glory!" Letting out a roar, Barbossa brought down the sword, stabbing it straight toward Jack's heart. There was barely a whisper as the sharp blade pierced the pirate's jacket and then an audible *tink* as steel met glass. Against his chest, Jack felt the glass bottle begin to vibrate. He opened his jacket. A small crack had appeared in the side of the bottle where it had been struck by Blackbeard's blade. As Jack watched, a few drops of water flowed out onto his shirt, like blood from a wound.

Jack looked up and smiled. "Ooh, Hector," he said,

hope long since lost to him finally returning, "I think my waters have broken."

As the twilight gave way to night, Jack ran toward the beach of Hangman's Bay, water pouring from the glass bottle and soaking his jacket. Just as he burst from the jungle onto the sand, Barbossa and his crew right behind him, the glass exploded into a thousand shards. The *Black Pearl* dropped at Jack's feet.

And then it began to grow.

And grow.

And grow.

Shimmying backward, Jack frantically tried to escape being trapped under the *Pearl.* His eyes were wide and his heart was pounding as he watched his beloved ship build back up.

And then it stopped growing.

Jack walked to it and leaned over. It *had* grown; that much was true. But while it was not a few inches long anymore, it now barely spanned a couple feet. It looked like a toy version of the real thing. Picking it up, Jack peered onto its decks. Then he lifted a foot as though trying to board. He sighed. "Maybe size does matter," he finally said sadly.

Barbossa took the ship from Jack. He stared at it for one long beat. In the light from the moon, the ship seemed like a fish out of water. Its sides seemed to heave for breath, its sails billowing in and out like gasping lungs. He walked with the *Pearl* to the edge of the water.

Then he threw it in.

"She needs the sea," Barbossa said, turning back to the gathered crowd.

Together, the two men stood on shore, watching the ship bobble on the waves. Then it began to sink, disappearing under the dark water. The pirates stared in shock, wondering what had gone wrong.

"She was a fine ship," Jack said after a moment.

"As fine as any that ever sailed," Barbossa agreed.

They stood in respectful silence, each lost in thoughts of the adventures he had had on the *Pearl*. Jack felt his heart breaking anew as, once more, his ship was taken from him. He hung his head.

"Something's happening." Henry's voice broke through the fog of sadness enveloping Jack. Slowly, Jack lifted his head. The boy was right. Something was indeed happening. In front of their very eyes, the sea began to bubble and foam. The water turned white, as though churned by some powerful force below. And then the *Pearl* exploded up from beneath the waves.

It was no longer the four-foot toy ship it had been only moments before. In the moonlight, its sides gleamed as though freshly polished. Its black sails hung from the masts and its Jolly Roger waved in the light wind off the sea. As it settled itself on the water, Jack smiled. The *Pearl* was back. And that meant so was he.

Chapter Thirteen

Unfortunately, Jack wasn't completely back. Not yet, at least. While the *Pearl* had returned, so, too, had the feud between him and Barbossa over who should captain it. And this round had gone to Barbossa—and his blasted monkey, freed along with the ship.

As the *Black Pearl* once again took to the ocean, the fastest ship at sea, Barbossa stood at its helm. On his shoulder, Jack the Monkey bared his teeth and let out a monkey laugh. Jack the pirate looked up from where he was being unceremoniously tied to the center mast, and scowled. He had never liked the foul creature. The monkey had an attitude. And it had only gotten worse since he had been stuck in the bottle.

"The course you sail must be exact, Captain," Jack heard Carina say. Straining his neck, he saw that she and Henry had also been tied to a mast. That, at least, gave him some pleasure.

Barbossa barely gave the girl a glance. His eyes were fixed in front of him, one hand on the wheel and a smug smile on his face. "There is no *exact* at sea!" he replied.

"You need to listen to her, Captain!" Henry pleaded. "She's the only one who can follow that X!"

That seemed to get Barbossa's attention. He looked down at the pair and raised an eyebrow. "Is that a fact?" he asked sarcastically. "This girl knows more of the sea than I?"

Carina ignored the jab. "You'll follow the Southern Cross to a single reflection point," she said. "I have a chronometer which determines longitude which will then take us to the *exact* spot at sea."

I do like a girl with a little bit of spunk, Jack thought, smiling. *Especially when that spunk comes in the form of proving Barbossa wrong.* He fidgeted with the ropes tying him to the mast, trying to loosen them. He knew that Carina was right and that she could find the X. He also knew that if he were still tied to the mast when that time came, he was unlikely to be the one to get the Trident. And if he was going to survive any future encounter with Salazar, he would need it.

As Jack struggled with his restraints, Barbossa stared long and hard at Carina. His eyes narrowed. She certainly seemed to know what she was talking about. He looked at Jack. Jack would never have brought her along if she couldn't be of some use to him. "Untie them!" he finally ordered. When Carina was free, he signaled her to join him at the helm. "Take the wheel, miss." The words were clearly hard for him to say. It was a known fact that having a woman on board was bad luck. And it was even worse luck for a woman to captain a ship. But he thought as he turned and looked behind them, spotting the *Silent Mary* in swift pursuit, that she was the best bet he had for surviving. He would let Carina follow her star. If he didn't, they were all going to die together anyway.

Carina raised her head. In the sky, the Southern Cross twinkled brightly, leading the way toward the destination only she could see. Henry stood beside her, and she sensed him following her gaze. The young man had been oddly quiet since they had been untied and she had taken the wheel from Barbossa. She wondered if he was thinking of his father. That was often where her thoughts went when night fell. That night, however, her thoughts were darker in nature.

"This ship . . . those ghosts," she said softly, breaking the silence between them. "There can be no logical explanation."

Henry tore his gaze from the sky and looked at her. "The myths of the sea are real, Carina. I'm glad you can see you were wrong."

"Wrong?" Carina repeated the word, letting it hang

between them for a long moment. Henry shifted nervously on his feet. Perhaps that had not been the right thing to say. He saw Carina's eyes narrow, and yet the corner of her mouth lifted as though she was trying not to smile. "Perhaps I had some doubts—thought you were mad." She paused. "One *could* say I was possibly, arguably a *bit* . . ." Her voice trailed off.

"Wrong," Henry finally said when it was clear she wouldn't say it herself. "The word is 'wrong.'"

"Slightly in error," Carina countered, her eyes sparkling.

"This is the worst apology I've ever heard," Henry observed. He got the feeling that she was teasing him—and enjoying it.

Carina cocked her head. "Apology?" she asked as though she were confused. "Why would I apologize?"

Henry gestured around him. "Because we've been chased by the dead; sail on a ship raised from a bottle! Where is your science in that?" *I've got her there!* Henry thought.

"It was *science* which found that map!" Carina said, not backing down.

Henry shook his head. "No," he replied. "*We* found it. Together."

"Fine," Carina said, looking down at the helm and studying it with feigned interest. "Then I will apologize. Although . . . one could argue that *you* owe *me* an apology, as my life has been threatened by pirates and dead men."

Henry stared at Carina for a beat. She was incorrigible with her teasing. He knew when to wave the white flag. "I'm going to the lookout," he announced, walking away with a small smile on his lips.

Behind him, Carina watched him go and grinned, pleased with herself. Turning back around, she was surprised to see Barbossa standing in the shadows. Stepping forward, he started to say something but stopped when he spotted Galileo's diary clutched in her hand. His eyes narrowed. "Where did you get that book, missy?" he asked. "I know this book."

"I would doubt you have read Galileo's diary," Carina snipped.

The pirate's long fingers reached out and gently brushed over the spot where the ruby had once been. "This book be pirate treasure," he said softly, "stolen from an Italian ship many years ago."

"Stolen?" Carina repeated. "You're mistaken."

Barbossa shook his head. "There was a ruby on the cover I would not soon forget."

Carina reached into her pocket and pulled out the ruby. Barbossa's eyes grew wide as the red gem caught the moonlight and twinkled. "This was given to me by my father," Carina said, holding out the ruby, "who was clearly a man of science."

Before she could stop him, Jack the Monkey grabbed the ruby. He squealed and placed it in Barbossa's open palm. "He was clearly a common *thief*," the pirate said, correcting her.

Carina slapped Barbossa. How dare he defile her father's name? The man knew nothing of him. He knew nothing of who he had been or what he had possibly suffered during his life. Her heart ached at the mere thought of her father's being anything but the man she had always imagined he was—a good, kind man with a scientific mind. A man who had suffered terribly at the loss of his daughter. A man who would have hated to know she had suffered even a day while she was alone in that orphanage. She clutched the diary to her heart. "This is my birthright," she said, "left with me on the steps of a children's home along with a name. Nothing more."

Expecting the pirate to laugh at her outburst, Carina was surprised when Barbossa instead took a step back, an unreadable expression crossing his face. "Oh, so you're an orphan," he said. He looked at her closely. "And what be you called?"

"The brightest star in the north gave me my name," she said cryptically.

"That would be Carina," Barbossa said.

His answer surprised her. She nodded slowly. "Carina Smyth," she said, introducing herself. "So you do know the stars?"

"I'm a captain," Barbossa said, his voice now soft and a touch sad. "I know which stars to follow home." Leaving Carina to mind the helm, Barbossa walked to the railing. His face was pale as he pulled the compass from his pocket and looked down at it. The needle shivered and then turned until it came to a stop—pointing straight at Carina.

Staggering backward, Barbossa nearly collided with the mast that still held Jack. The pirate had overheard the whole conversation and now looked up at his old friend and still older nemesis with a mischievous twinkle in his eye. "Smyth? Smyth? What an exotic name, Hector," he said, his voice playful. "Didn't we once know someone named Smyth? Don't tell me, it's coming to me . . . I'll pull the memory straight from the abyss. . . ."

"Be warned, Jack!" Barbossa growled.

Never one to heed a warning, Jack went on. He lifted a finger to his goatee and began to play with it. "I'm remembering the visage of a pretty young lass. A fair beauty with one undeniable flaw—you."

"Shut yer trap!"

Clearly Jack had hit a nerve. Still, he kept pressing, finding pleasure in Barbossa's obvious pain. "Now what was her name? The one you were revoltingly entwined with twenty years ago? She's on the tip of my tongue. . . ."

Barbossa drew his sword. "You're about to lose that tongue!" he warned, his hand tightening on the hilt.

"No, don't help me," Jack went on, unable to stop when he was having such fun. "I'll get it. It was a royal name—regal as the creature it adorned." He paused, letting the suspense—and torture—build. Then he let out a happy shout, as though he had only then remembered. "Margaret! Margaret *Smyth*! I can picture her as if she were standing in front of me!" Purposefully, he turned so he was looking right at Carina. Then he looked back at Barbossa. He could practically see the fire coming out of the man's ears. Jack had accomplished just what he had set out to—revealing Barbossa's connection to Carina—his *familial* connection. Not only had it been a fun game of sorts for Jack—after all, he really did love teasing his old friend—but more important, that connection gave Jack a very big bargaining chip. "So . . . shall we make an accord? Or should I tell Carina Smyth what we both know to be true?"

Barbossa leveled his sword at Jack's throat. "This secret we will take to our graves!"

"Kill me and you have nothing to bargain the dead with," Jack pointed out with a shrug. "You need me, Hector. The way a child needs a—"

"Silence!" Barbossa's voice rang out over the deck, startling a sleeping pirate and causing Carina to shoot the two men a look. Lowering his voice, Barbossa grabbed Jack by the throat. "Margaret died and I summoned as much honor as a worthless blackguard ever

could. I named the nursling myself. Placed her on the orphan steps, never to see her again. I thought the ruby would afford her some ease of life." He had never imagined that instead of using the gem on the diary to help her situation, Carina would make the scribblings *inside* her life's work. Nor could he ever have imagined that somehow that very obsession would lead her straight back to him—and make him vulnerable to Jack. "Tell me what you want."

Despite the fact that Barbossa's fingers were still tight around his neck, Jack smiled. "Well, let's see," he said gleefully. "I want my compass, your jacket, a lock of your hair, two hundred and sixteen barrels of rum . . . and the monkey."

"You want the monkey?" Barbossa said, surprised. He hadn't seen that one coming.

Jack nodded. "Yes. For dinner. And throw in the Trident, if you don't mind. Everyone else seems to—" Before he could finish, Jack the Monkey reached out and stuffed a dirty cloth in Jack's mouth, gagging him.

"No deal, Jack," Barbossa said, regaining his composure. "A clever girl such as that would never believe a swine like me could be her blood. The Trident will be mine!"

"Redcoats!"

Henry's frightened voice rang out. Both Barbossa and Jack craned their necks to see where the young man stood in the lookout. Even from a distance, they could see his face had turned ashen. He was pointing behind them.

Rushing to the rail, Barbossa looked out over the water. As the *Pearl* rose on a wave, he saw just what had given Henry such a fright—and rightly so. Coming on fast was the British warship *Essex*. Its cannons were at the ready, and he could make out marines rushing about the decks, preparing for battle. "She's come starboard!" Barbossa shouted, turning to his own men. "We'll fight to the last. The *Pearl* will *not* be taken from me again!"

Jack could do nothing but watch helplessly as

Barbossa began to bark orders. He struggled against the rope that held him tight to the mast. But the rope would not budge. Jack was going nowhere, which left him in a uniquely uncomfortable position to witness as the *Essex* moved closer and closer until it was within firing distance. Then he watched as thirty cannons on the *Essex* were lit and aimed at the *Pearl*. Over the waves, Jack heard the unmistakable voice of Lieutenant Scarfield as he shouted, "Prepare to fire."

Jack started to squint his eyes shut but stopped as he spotted something moving up behind the *Essex*. He realized the *Pearl* was not going to be destroyed—not by the *Essex*, anyway. For there, rising out of the waves like a great toothed sea creature, was the *Silent Mary*. As Jack watched, her hull opened wide and then, with a loud groan, snapped down, breaking the *Essex* in half. The British warship didn't stand a chance. It exploded from within, the barrels of gunpowder that had been readied to destroy the *Pearl* igniting all at once.

Bursting through the wreckage, the *Silent Mary* continued to sail toward them. Barbossa stood, his hand on the railing, the fire from the *Essex* reflected in his eyes. Quickly he turned and rushed to the helm. Carina was holding on to the wheel, but barely. Her fingers shook as she took in the carnage the *Silent Mary* had wrought.

"Whatever happens," Barbossa said, trying to calm her, "stay your course!"

She looked up at him, her eyes wide. He worried she was going to faint, or scream, or do something equally silly. But to his surprise, she simply nodded and lifted her head back to the stars. Turning, Barbossa hid a smile. It seemed it was not just a love of the stars the young woman had gotten from her father.

Chapter Fourteen

Captain Salazar was pleased. He had destroyed the *Essex* as if it were no more than a flea beneath his foot. And now he was about to take the *Black Pearl* and, with it, Jack the Sparrow.

Jumping onto the deck of the *Pearl,* sword at his side and death in his eyes, he stared around at the pirates. *Sorry lot,* he thought as he took the men in. Their clothes were a mess and not one was in a uniform. Some didn't even have shoes. And as he looked at the wood beneath him, he observed that clearly no one had done a thorough cleaning of the *Pearl*'s deck in years. Those pitiful excuses for seamen deserved to die. But not before one pirate in particular met his demise.

"We've come with the butcher's bill!" As he spoke,

his ghostly crew joined him on the *Pearl*. "Where is Jack the Sparrow?"

Stepping forward, Barbossa drew his own sword. "We'll fight to the end!" he shouted bravely. Unfortunately, not all his men seemed to agree with him. He heard splashing as some jumped overboard. Others tried to fight the ghosts but stood no chance. Screams echoed over the *Pearl* as those men were slain where they stood.

"Where is he?" Salazar asked again.

"Tied to the mast!" Mullroy cried.

Barbossa turned and shot the weaselly man a look. The man shrugged.

All eyes turned toward the mast.

Jack wasn't there.

He was, thanks to Henry's quick thinking and fast rope cutting, now aboard the *Silent Mary*. Salazar saw the pirate jauntily waving to him from the ship.

"Leave him to me!" Salazar said to his men. He sprinted across the deck, stepped up onto the railing, and then leapt across the water that separated the two ships. He landed on a cannon beside Jack, his sword already drawn and ready.

Jack met him with his own sword drawn. As the two men began to parry along the side of the ship, it became clear that Salazar was the stronger swordsman. His blade whipped through the air with frightening ferocity, slicing anything that got in its way—ropes, canvases, the occasional wick of a cannon. Trying to escape, Jack began leaping from cannon to cannon. But Salazar stayed with him leap for leap.

"I will break you this time," Salazar said, his voice as cold as the dead blood that flowed through his veins, "punish you for the pain I must endure, feeling my own death over and over."

"Or you could simply forgive me," Jack suggested. Looking over his shoulder, he saw that the *Pearl* had floated close enough to the *Silent Mary* that he could jump onto it. Quickly, he did just that. Salazar followed.

On board the *Pearl,* all hell had broken loose.

Pirates were fighting ghosts. Jack saw Henry desperately trying to keep Carina safe while she, in turn, tried to save Barbossa, whose peg leg had gotten stuck in a hole. As Jack watched, Barbossa tried to duck out of the way of a ghost's sword but failed. He let out a roar as the sword slashed his side. Jack also spotted his old crew among the pirates. It looked like they had escaped the redcoats on a rowboat in the confusion and had boarded the *Pearl*. Gibbs and Scrum were standing back to back as they tried to keep the ghosts at bay, the uncharacteristically clever tactic working well. Jack opened his mouth to welcome his men back to the *Pearl* but stopped when Salazar's sword swung down, missing him by mere inches. With a cry, Jack leapt back onto the *Silent Mary*.

"You took everything from me!" Salazar shouted, following him. "Made me more repulsive than any pirate!"

"That's not necessarily true," Jack said. "Have you

ever met Edward the Blue? He's very repulsive. The way he eats . . ." His voice trailed off as a loud wrenching sound pierced the air. Looking at the front of the ship, he saw that the carved female figurehead on the *Silent Mary*'s bow was slowly coming to life. The figurehead detached herself from the ship and climbed over the rail, then stood towering over Jack. "That's very strange," Jack said. "But I do like your dress."

In answer, the figurehead let out a horrifying scream.

Jack screamed back—and took off running.

Behind him, the figurehead raised a sword and went on the attack. Stuck between Salazar and the figurehead, Jack desperately tried to fight his way free. But no matter how fast he moved, the strange, horrific pair kept coming. Ducking in front of a cannon, Jack tried to catch his breath only to watch Salazar light the cannon. Just before it fired, Jack swung it up and over so it was no longer pointed right in his face. Instead, when it went off, it blew the figurehead's face completely apart. But still she kept attacking, angrier than ever. Behind him Salazar stood, blocking any escape.

Raising her sword high above her, the figurehead was about to finish off Jack when there was a loud crunching sound. In front of his very eyes, she was squashed between the bow of the *Pearl* and the side of the *Silent Mary* as they collided. The momentum threw Jack to the deck. Looking up, he found himself staring right into the very angry eyes of Salazar. The ghost lifted his sword high. Jack gulped.

And then dawn broke over the horizon.

"Land!"

The cry startled both Salazar and Jack motionless. Slowly, they turned and looked over the railing of the *Black Pearl*. Sure enough, an island had appeared, seemingly out of thin air. Jack couldn't help smiling. Carina Smyth had done it. She had found the X.

Then his eyes grew wide as he realized that not only had she found the X, but she was about to sail the

Black Pearl right onto it! Salazar seemed to reach that conclusion at the same time. He looked down at Jack and then back at the rapidly approaching island. Jack knew the captain wasn't stupid. If he didn't return to the *Mary* and avoid dry land, he would die again—and this time, he would not come back.

With an angry shout, Salazar began to back up. But before he leapt onto the *Mary*, he reached out, trying to grab hold of Carina, who had made her way closer to Jack. His fingers were just about to close around the girl's wrist when Henry leapt in between them. Salazar grabbed him instead, and as the *Pearl* ran aground, he hauled Henry aboard the *Mary*. With a groan, the ghost ship veered away, just barely missing the island.

Aboard the *Pearl*, Jack, Barbossa, and Carina watched as the other ship retreated to the sea.

"Henry!" Carina shouted. "We have to go back for Henry!"

Beside her, Barbossa shook his head. There was no going back. "The Trident is the only thing that can save him now," he said, surprised by the sadness he felt at Carina's possible loss. *So we'd better hope we can find it,* he added silently, *or Henry is as good as dead.*

I might as well be dead, Henry thought as he stared around at the ghosts who had gathered to see the *Silent Mary*'s newest prisoner. *There is no way I'm getting out of this mess. I'll go to a watery grave by the hand of Salazar or, worse, one of his crew, and then I'll never save my father . . . or see Carina again.* He sighed, feeling the tight ropes burn his wrists and ankles. It was going to take a miracle to get him free, and Henry was pretty sure he had used up all his miracles trying to find Carina and Jack.

As Captain Salazar approached, his dead men stood at attention.

"*Capitan,* Jack Sparrow is going for the Trident!" one of the ghost crewmen cried. "He's on dry land; there is nothing we can do."

Lifting his head, Henry tried to find Carina on the

shore of the island. From his spot on the *Silent Mary,* he saw now that the island was more rock than beach. Dark stones formed from countless lava spills dotted the small strip of beach and rose into the hills, giving the whole island an air of desolation and dark despair. Henry shuddered at the thought of Carina there, with only Jack and Barbossa and their respective crews as company. He hoped she was okay.

"I took this boy for a reason." Henry jumped at Salazar's words, which pulled Henry's attention back to his own dire situation. "I will walk in his shoes. No pirate will defeat us!"

Walk in his shoes? Henry repeated in his head. Whatever that meant, it did not sound good.

Evidently, Salazar's men knew exactly what he meant. The ghastly crew members looked at one another, understanding dawning on their faces.

"But once you possess the living, there is no coming back. You will be trapped in his body forever!" said another ghost.

Possess the living? Henry looked around frantically. There had to be some means of escape, something he had not thought of.

Then Henry met Salazar's gaze dead in the eye. "The Trident will set me free," the ghost captain said with a wicked smile. "Time to kill the Sparrow."

Chapter Fifteen

Carina was beginning to believe her luck had run out. She found herself staring down at nothing more than a rocky landmass. That was where the Map No Man Can Read led? From her spot on the deck of the *Pearl*, she looked over the deserted island and sighed. "It's empty," she said softly. "But this has to be it."

Turning her back to the beach, she lowered her head. What cruel trick of fate was this, to come this far and not find what they were looking for? As she tried to wrap her head around the horrible realization that maybe, just maybe, she had been wrong all along, the first ray of daylight appeared on the horizon. Behind her, she heard one of Jack's men give an excited shout. Whipping around, her eyes grew wide.

In the light, the rocks revealed their secret. Thousands of diamonds sparkled, embedded in the volcanic rock, ripe for the picking.

"We're rich!" another pirate cried out, jumping down from the *Pearl* and racing to the rocks. Bending down, he began to pull at one of the larger diamonds, trying to free it from the rock.

Just as he managed to do so, there was a huge roar, and a blast of scorching hot steam shot up from a crack in the rocks. As Carina watched, the crack grew wider and wider. The pirate who had pulled the diamond free now let out a shout of terror as he was pulled violently down beneath the earth. Where he had once stood, an empty space remained.

"Back to the ship!" Gibbs shouted, pushing his way through the crowd of pirates who had hoped to finally get their treasure. As they ran, more light broke over the horizon, and suddenly, the entire island was flooded with light. Hitting the diamonds, the light caused them to shimmer and sparkle.

Carina stepped forward, her earlier disappointment fading. "Look at it, Jack," she said in a whisper. "It's the most beautiful thing I've ever seen."

Jack shrugged. "Beautiful rocks," he said, unimpressed, "that kill for no reason."

"Not rocks, Jack," Carina said, correcting him. "Stars." Quickly, she began to climb down from the *Pearl*.

Behind her, Jack and Barbossa exchanged looks. Had she said *stars*? What were stars doing on an island? Confused and curious, Jack followed the girl. Barbossa followed a step later, not willing to let Carina out of his sight for too long.

"Stars and planets exactly as they appear in the sky," Carina said as she made her way closer. "This island is a perfect reflection of the heavens."

"But it's still rocks," Jack pointed out. "*Murderous* rocks!"

Carina ignored the pirate and kept walking, her mind spinning as the truth began to reveal itself more fully. She hadn't been wrong. This island was what she had been looking for all along. And if the rest of her calculations were correct—which she had no doubt now that they were—when they found the missing star, they would find the X.

Unaware that both Barbossa and Jack were watching her, Carina followed the familiar patterns of the sky. As she walked over the diamonds, it seemed almost as though she were walking across the night sky. Turning to Barbossa, Jack put a sympathetic hand on the man's shoulder. Clearly, his newfound daughter had a marble or two loose. He felt it only right to give the man the other bad news. "Hector," he said, his voice serious, "I think you should know . . . she's a horologist."

Barbossa silenced Jack with a look. Then he turned back to Carina. She had stopped at a particular spot and was looking back and forth between the ground in front of her and the diary in her hand. "Finish it, Carina," he said, realizing that she was staring at a cluster of five jewels—not diamonds, but vibrant rubies—formed to create a constellation identical to the sketch in the diary. And yet one of the rubies did not glow like the others. Carina knew exactly what she was supposed to do.

She took the ruby from her pocket and held it up. "For my father," Carina said, unaware of the flash of sadness that flickered across Barbossa's face. Then she removed the dull rock and placed her ruby down in the middle of the constellation. It slid into place, a perfect fit. "X marks the spot!" Carina said as the jems in the ground suddenly lit up, forming the shape of the Trident. A rumbling seemed to start deep within the island.

Just before a giant crack opened beneath her feet, Jack reached out and pulled Carina away. They stood a few feet away and watched as the world began to break apart—literally. In between the bed of diamonds and the *Pearl*, the beach gave way to water. Invisible winds tore at the water, causing waves to rush in opposite directions, parting the sea in front of their very eyes.

The water rose up, up, and up from the ocean floor until it surrounded them and revealed the bottom of the sea.

Looking down, Jack had only a moment to realize what was about to happen. He told Carina to hang on before the sand beneath their feet gave way, and they slipped and slid down a wall of water until they landed, with a thud, on the ocean floor hundreds of feet below. All around them, the water hung like curtains, unfortunate fish, caught in the wrong place at the wrong time, suspended for a moment between sea and air before dropping to the ground, where they flopped about, gasping the unexpected air helplessly. With wide eyes, Jack looked around at what no man—no living man—had ever seen before. He spotted dozens of shipwrecks, the ships' sides worn through and covered in barnacles. He even spotted a giant blue whale as it swam around the hole. "The back side of water," Jack said. "Don't see that every day." Then, noticing that Carina's diary had fallen to the sea floor, Jack picked it up and pocketed it.

"Jack, there it is!" Carina's voice caught the pirate's

attention, and he turned. She was staring at a shell-shaped chamber in front of them. Made of coral and sea glass, it rose from the ocean floor. And in the middle of it, in all its mythical glory, was the Trident. Nearly eight feet tall, with three sharp prongs that managed to reflect light even down in the depths of the hole, the Trident of Poseidon oozed with absolute power. It was an object ancient and strong, with an undeniable pull on the two mortals who now stood staring at it. As if in a trance, Jack and Carina took a step forward.

"Jack!"

Snapping out of it, Jack and Carina turned around. To their surprise, they saw Henry coming toward them.

"Henry!" Carina cried, joy flooding her face.

But Henry didn't stop. He pushed past Carina, the force throwing her to the ocean floor. He took out his sword and swung it—right at Jack. The pirate ducked out of the way, just barely avoiding being impaled by the boy's smooth and well-practiced swings.

Jack cocked his head. Smooth and well-practiced?

Last time he had been in a sword fight with Henry, the boy could barely lift the sword without his arm shaking. He narrowed his eyes and watched as Henry came at him again. "Arms straight . . . shoulders square . . . front leg bent . . ." he observed with growing suspicion.

"Henry?" Carina cried out again, pushing herself to her feet.

Jack shook his head. "Henry doesn't hold a sword like that," he said. Lighting fast, Jack pulled out a small dagger from his boot and sliced the boy's arm. As Jack watched, Henry looked down and touched the blood that welled up on his skin. Then he looked back up at Jack. But the eyes that bore into Jack with rage and pain were no longer Henry's. They were unmistakably those of Captain Salazar. Jack gulped. Salazar had taken over Henry's body—which meant, unfortunately for Jack, that he could now walk on land.

"Cut me and you cut the boy," Salazar said in Henry's voice, proving Jack's suspicions right.

"Definitely not Henry!" Jack shouted as Salazar/ Henry once again came at him, fighting with all the pent-up rage and anger he had bottled over the years. He knocked the dagger out of Jack's hand and reached for him, his fingers clawing for Jack's neck.

"Leave him!" Carina's voice startled Salazar and stopped him. Looking over, he saw that she was holding the Trident, the tip pointed at Henry. "Drop your sword!"

"Carina . . ." Jack warned. He knew the girl had only just come to grips with the otherworldly and their ilk. He could tell she was having a hard time believing that the boy in front of her was anyone but the boy she had come to know and perhaps, Jack suspected, love. But Henry was just a vessel, controlled by Salazar, who would do anything to get what he wanted. And what he wanted was the Trident.

In one swift movement, Salazar rushed Carina, knocking the Trident out of her hand. As she once more fell to the ground, Salazar closed his hand around the ancient weapon. With a triumphant cry, he lifted it into the air. "It's over, Jack!"

The Trident glowed, the full power of the ancient staff eager to be released after thousands of years. The ground beneath Jack's feet began to shake, and the water, already torn apart in an unnatural way, flowed straight up, rising in front of his very eyes. Wind whipped along the floor of the ocean as it, too, began to rise.

Jack gulped as everything went upside down and topsy-turvy. It did, indeed, seem like things for him—and perhaps the rest of civilization—were about to get very, very strange.

Salazar felt the power rushing through him, the feeling greater than any he had ever known. Killing pirates paled in comparison to the feeling. Watching Jack squirm, while still satisfying, was a mere trifle compared to the sensations. With every passing second, Salazar felt the Trident giving him more and more strength until, with a triumphant cry, he was able to free himself from Henry's body. As the boy fell to the ground, half-conscious and wounded, Salazar stepped forward. In the murky half-light of the ocean floor, his ghostly form looked even more ghastly. But he didn't care. Now he was nigh unstoppable, a god among these poor mortals.

"Hola, Sparrow," he said. Then he pointed the Trident at Jack and, with a flick of his wrist, sent Jack flying against a large rock.

Carina rushed over to the half-conscious form lying on the sandy floor.

"Henry!" She dropped to her knees and shook him. Nothing happened. "Wake up!" She shook him again. Still, nothing happened. Her eyes lifted to the curtain of water that surrounded them. Behind the curtain, unable to cross over into the clearing, were a dozen or so of Salazar's crew. They stood, shimmering eerily, taunting her in ghostly whispers. Ignoring them, Carina cupped her hands, gathered some of the salty liquid, and then dumped it on Henry. "*Wake up!* He's killing Jack!"

Ever so slowly, Henry opened his eyes. In a daze, he looked around, unable to wrap his head around his new surroundings. Finally, his unfocused gaze met Carina's frightened one. "The Trident," she said, seeing that she had his attention—sort of. "Salazar can walk on land with the Trident." That fact had only just occurred to her. It explained everything: how Salazar could be fighting Jack while his men stayed trapped in the water. "Everyone knows ghosts can't walk on land!" she cried, suddenly an expert on the paranormal.

As the true power of the Trident became clear to Carina, her eyes widened and she glanced at Salazar, who continued to torture Jack, throwing him in and out of the water as though he were skipping rocks. Struggling to sit up, Henry, too, looked at the old enemies. "The power of the sea . . ." Henry whispered.

Carina's breath caught in her throat. That was it! The cryptic message she had translated in her prison cell. "'To release the power of the sea, all must divide,'" she repeated aloud.

Henry looked at her, confused. "Divide?" he said. His head still hurt and he was having a hard time focusing.

Carina nodded. "If the Trident holds all the power—"

"Then every curse is held inside . . ." Henry finished, finally beginning to see—and think—clearly. "Divide!" he said. It all made sense. They had to divide the Trident. They had to *break* it. If they could do that, all the curses of the sea would be broken, including Salazar's—and he would be mortal again.

Unaware that Henry and Carina had found a potential way to destroy him once and for all, Salazar continued to play with Jack like a cat playing with a mouse. Lifting the Trident, he hurled Jack into a large coral reef. Despite the obvious pain Jack was in, he struggled to his feet. "Surrender," he said, his words echoing those of his nineteen-year-old self, "and I'll let you live."

Salazar snarled. "You want me to surrender?"

"I highly recommend it," Jack said tauntingly. Behind Salazar, he saw Henry push himself to his feet. He and the boy exchanged one small, subtle nod. Then Jack looked back at Salazar—just in time to watch him plunge the Trident straight into Jack's chest.

In the moment that followed, everything stopped.

The wind ceased howling.

The water appeared to still.

As Henry and Carina stood watching, their mouths froze open.

And then Salazar smiled. His hand tightened on the end of the Trident, which he still held. "Jack Sparrow is no more."

Looking down at where the pointed end of the Trident had pierced his chest, Jack was quiet for one moment. Slowly, he lifted both his hands and grasped the shaft right behind the prongs. Then he, too, smiled. "I'm pretty sure this was part of the plan."

Salazar's eyes narrowed. "And what plan was that?"

In answer, Jack opened his bloody shirt, revealing Galileo's diary. The sharpest point of the Trident had gone straight through it, stopping just short of piercing Jack's heart. And though he had not gone completely unscathed—the prongs had cut him deeply—he would live. Looking over his shoulder, Jack gave out a shout. *"Henry! Be the last to die, mate!"*

Salazar turned his head, but it was too late. While he had been focused on destroying Jack, Henry had gotten to his feet and pulled his sword. At Jack's signal, he swung it down with all his strength. There was a loud clang as the steel of his sword met the metal of the Trident, and then the ancient weapon shattered into a thousand pieces.

As the fragments dropped, one by one, to the sea floor, Jack's wound began to heal. Together, Henry and

Jack turned toward Salazar. In front of their very eyes, they saw the captain begin to transform. His skin grew less translucent. The hole in his skull slowly filled in. His uniform, for so long bloodied and stained, became clean and perfect. In mere moments, he was a ghost no longer. Now Captain Salazar, in all his glory, stood in front of them, looking as though not a day had passed in all those long, horrible years.

Salazar's curse had been broken.

Chapter Sixteen

"All curses are broken—which means my luck has returned!"

Jack's happy shout quickly turned to a groan as he watched the walls of water, kept at bay because of the curse, begin to buckle with its absence. Perhaps his luck hadn't completely returned.

"Run!"

Carina's voice cut through the noise of the rushing water. Jack didn't hesitate. Pushing Henry forward, he took off after Carina, who had already begun to run up the side of a coral reef. The prickly staircase to the surface was rapidly being covered in water. They didn't have much time.

"The *Pearl*!" Jack shouted, pointing above them.

All eyes turned upward. There, hovering on the rim of the parted ocean, was the *Black Pearl*. The ship's anchor had been thrown overboard and was hanging down in the abyss. On it, holding out his hand, was Barbossa.

"Hurry!" he cried as the walls of water continued to cave in.

Just in time, Jack, Carina, and Henry reached the large anchor. After they threw themselves onto it, Barbossa shouted up to the pirates on the *Pearl* to pull.

But they were not the only ones who had seen a way out of the water. Beneath them, Salazar and a few of his now living men had grabbed on to the bottom of the anchor. Pulling themselves up, arm over arm, the men began to climb toward the others as the water swirled around them.

Up on the *Pearl,* the pirates struggled to pull the anchor up. But between all the people clinging to it and the heavy current, they couldn't. The ship began to tip.

"She's giving way!" Henry shouted.

"Climb!" Barbossa ordered.

As fast as they could, Jack and Henry began to pull

themselves up. Behind them, Carina struggled, the weight of her dress making it harder for her to move. The *Pearl* tipped further, knocking Carina off balance. She screamed as her hands slipped. But just as she was about to fall, she felt strong, rough fingers close around her hand. As she looked up, her eyes met Barbossa's. "I've got you," he said, his shirt sleeve slipping back, revealing his forearm.

Carina's breath caught in her throat. And suddenly, she was no longer thinking about the terrifying fact that her feet dangled helplessly over the sea floor below and Salazar and his men were moving ever closer to her. All Carina could see, all she could think about, was the tattoo revealed on Barbossa's arm: the tattoo of five stars clustered together—the tattoo that meant *Carina*. Her eyes once again met Barbossa's. "What am I to you?" she whispered, though she believed she knew the answer. The truth was there, marked on his skin for her to see.

Barbossa stared at her, his face softening and his

eyes clear. "Treasure," he said simply. And then, making sure she was safely on the anchor, he grabbed the sword from Jack's belt and let himself fall.

Carina screamed as she watched the pirate, her father, fall through the air, the sword in his hand slicing through Salazar's men. And then, in one last—or perhaps first—act of fatherly love, he fell onto Salazar, stabbing the man in his now beating heart. Together, the pair plummeted back to the sea floor. As Barbossa looked up, his eyes locked on Carina's and he smiled, content at last.

A moment later, the water rushed over him and he, along with Salazar and his men, disappeared from view.

"Hang on!" Henry cried as the anchor, now freed from most of the weight, began to rise rapidly. Just as the hole in the sea completely collapsed, the anchor burst through the surface of the water and flew into the air, where it hung, with Jack, Henry, and Carina clinging to it like wet barnacles, next to the *Black Pearl*. They had made it.

But the cost had been high.

The trio dropped from the anchor onto the deck of the *Black Pearl* and lay there for a moment, coughing and trying to catch their breath. When Jack was sure all the water was out of his lungs, he stood up and moved to the railing of the *Pearl*. In the sky, the clouds disappeared, letting the sun burst through, and below, the sea turned calm.

As the rest of the *Pearl*'s crew joined him, Jack removed his hat and held it to his heart. "A pirate's life, Hector," he said softly. It was hard to imagine life at sea without his old friend. But as Jack turned and looked at Carina, he couldn't help smiling. The old man had left a legacy, something only a rare pirate did.

Carina had no idea that Jack was looking at her. Standing beside Henry, she stared out at the calm sea. She was surprised that it could be so beautiful when only moments earlier it had been so deadly. What surprised her even more was the depth of her sadness as she thought of the man whom she had not known for very long at all, the man who had sacrificed his life for hers.

"Are you okay?" Henry asked gently.

She sighed. "For a moment, I had everything, Henry, only to lose it all again."

"Not everything, Ms. Smyth," Henry replied. He handed her the diary. Then, slowly, he reached out and took her other hand, interlocking his fingers with hers. Before she could overthink it, she threw herself into his arms and squeezed him with all her might. He was right: she hadn't lost everything. In fact, she realized as she felt Henry's arms tighten around her and pull her closer that she had maybe even gained something more.

"Barbossa," she said, correcting him. "My name is Barbossa."

Chapter Seventeen

As the sun set over the Caribbean Sea, the orange light illuminated the giant cliffs that rose out of the water. The cliffs had not changed in hundreds of years. They were the same as they had been all those years earlier when Will Turner had said his first good-bye to Elizabeth Swann before returning to the *Dutchman*. They were the same as they had been when Elizabeth had returned ten years later to introduce Henry to his father. And they were the same as they had been when Henry set off on his adventure, the cliffs standing watch behind him.

Now the *Black Pearl* was sailing away toward its next adventure. Standing on top of the bluffs, looking out to sea, Henry felt nervous and excited at the same time. Glancing next to him, he realized it wasn't just because he might see his father. In the setting sun, Carina looked almost ethereal. The rays of light made her hair sparkle and her eyes shine. Realizing he was staring at her, she flushed becomingly.

"Maybe Jack was right," Henry said, breaking their companionable silence.

"About what?" Carina asked.

"The unscratchable itch," he replied. Before she could ask him what that was, he leaned in and parted his lips. His eyes closed and his breath caught as he moved to kiss her, eager to feel the softness of her lips. . . .

Slap!

Instead, he felt the palm of Carina's hand.

"What are you doing?" he cried, lifting his hand to his stinging cheek.

"Just making sure it's truly you," she said, a small playful smile tugging at her lips.

Henry grinned. "It's me—still me!"

"Then I guess I was . . ."

"Wrong!" Henry filled in for her, their first argument back on the *Pearl* replaying. But then Henry had been unsure of his feelings. Now he had no doubt.

"*Slightly* in error," Carina said teasingly. "Although one could argue—"

Henry stopped Carina mid-argument with a kiss. Soft at first, it grew in intensity as they both let go of their reservations and admitted that Jack had, indeed, been right. Henry finally pulled away. He tucked a wisp of Carina's hair behind her ear. "Apology accepted," he said, going in for another kiss only to be stopped. Not by a slap this time, but by something he saw out of the corner of his eye. "Do you see that?" he asked, walking to the edge of the cliff.

Following him, Carina looked over the open ocean. At first she saw nothing but the rolling waves and a few birds flapping in the wind. But then, on the horizon, she saw a flash of something. Small at first, it became larger, moving straight toward them as though blasted from the sun itself. Beside her, Henry pulled out his telescope and, with shaking hands, lifted it to his eyes. Then he let out a cry.

The *Dutchman* had returned!

Will Turner had never thought this day would come. He was alive. His curse was broken. He no longer had to spend his days trapped on the *Dutchman*. He could once again walk on land whenever he chose. And best of all, he could finally see Henry again. He disembarked the ship and climbed the cliffs, the most important place in the world to him. When he'd made it to the top, he watched as his son and a beautiful girl quickly made their way toward him.

"Let me look at you, Son," Will said when Henry stopped in front of him. He put his hands on the boy's shoulders and smiled. *Man's shoulders,* he thought, correcting himself. For Henry was no longer the little boy he had left years earlier. Nor was he the headstrong and naive boy who had come to his ship and vowed to save him. Whatever events had unfolded to bring them both to that point and break the curse had changed Henry. The boy was gone, replaced by the handsome man who now stood in front of him. Unable to contain his emotions any longer, Will pulled Henry into an embrace. They stood there for a long time, reunited and unwilling to let go quite yet.

Finally, Will pushed Henry back. "How did you do it?" The question had been preoccupying him ever since he had felt the curse lift. "How did you save me?"

Henry looked at his father and then at Carina. "Let me tell you a story," he began, "a tale of the greatest treasure any man can hold. . . ." And as he started his story, Henry couldn't help smiling, for he knew now that treasure wasn't just gold and gems. Treasure was family and love. And he had both.

The Ending's End

Jack was back where he belonged. Standing on the *Pearl,* he stared at the shore through his spyglass. Scanning the land before him, he paused as he spotted Carina and Henry. They kissed.

"That is a truly revolting sight," he said under his breath.

"Captain Jack Sparrow on deck!"

Gibbs's cry pulled Jack's attention away from the lovers. Jack smiled. *Captain.* It sounded good to hear that said with respect again. He turned to Gibbs. Behind them, the cliffs were fading into the distance as they sailed toward the setting sun. They were surrounded by nothing but open ocean. There were no cursed sailors after them, no British warships moving up behind, no ghost sharks attacking at port or starboard. Just the sea. Just the way Jack liked it.

"What be our heading, sir?" Gibbs asked.

"We will follow the stars, Gibbs," he finally said. "I have a rendezvous beyond my beloved horizon."

As Jack turned, Jack the Monkey landed on his shoulder. The pirate nearly tossed him overboard but stopped when he saw that the monkey was holding something in his paws. Lifting his paws, the monkey dropped Jack's compass into his palm. Then he pulled back his lips in a monkey smile.

Flipping open the compass, Jack looked down at its needle. As it slowly turned toward the horizon, Jack began to hum a tune under his breath. The compass no longer needed to point in any one direction, letting Jack know that he finally had all he'd ever wanted. He was back aboard the *Black Pearl,* and now he had only the infinite delight of the sea to look forward to. He was living the best life, the only life he could ever have wanted—the pirate's life.